He was here as a cop, not as a man.

But it was as a man that he was reacting. And when the wind conspired against him, suddenly gliding her hair against his skin, making all hell break out inside of him, he felt as if he was fighting a losing battle.

But curiosity and desire got the better of him. He gave in to the former, did his damnedest to reconstruct the latter—and kissed her.

There had been many missteps in Brady Coltrane's life.

At night, he would lie awake at times and review them. Thinking how different the course of his existence might be if he had just done some things differently. Even one thing differently.

And now this could be added to the list. Because until he kissed Patience, he didn't know. Didn't know that this woman could break apart his carefully constructed fortress.

Dear Reader,

Winter may be cold, but the reading's hot here at Silhouette Intimate Moments, starting with the latest CAVANAUGH JUSTICE tale from award winner Marie Ferrarella, *Alone in the Dark*. Take one tough cop on a mission of protection, add one warmhearted veterinarian, shake, stir, and...voilà! The perfect romance to curl up with as the snow falls.

Karen Templeton introduces the first of THE MEN OF MAYES COUNTY in *Everybody's Hero*—and trust me, you really will fall for Joe Salazar and envy heroine Taylor McIntyre for getting to go home with him at the end of the day. FAMILY SECRETS: THE NEXT GENERATION concludes with *In Destiny's Shadow*, by Ingrid Weaver, and you'll definitely want to be there for the slam-bang finish of the continuity, not to mention the romance with a twist. Those SPECIAL OPS are back in Lyn Stone's *Under the Gun*, an on-the-run story guaranteed to set your heart racing. Linda O. Johnston shows up *Not a Moment Too Soon* to tell the story of a desperate father turning to the psychic he once loved to search for his kidnapped daughter. Finally, welcome new author Rosemary Heim, whose debut novel, *Virgin in Disguise*, has a bounty hunter falling for her quarry—with passionate consequences.

Enjoy all six of these terrific books, then come back next month for more of the best and most exciting romance reading around—only from Silhouette Intimate Moments.

Enjoy!

Leslie J. Wainger
Excecutive Editor

Please address questions and book requests to:
Silhouette Reader Service
U.S.: 3010 Walden Ave., P.O. Box 1325, Buffalo, NY 14269
Canadian: P.O. Box 609, Fort Erie, Ont. L2A 5X3

Alone in the Dark

MARIE FERRARELLA

♥ *Silhouette*®

INTIMATE MOMENTS™

Published by Silhouette Books

America's Publisher of Contemporary Romance

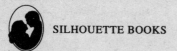 **SILHOUETTE BOOKS**

ISBN 0-373-27397-5

ALONE IN THE DARK

Copyright © 2004 by Marie Rydzynski-Ferrarella

Visit Silhouette Books at www.eHarlequin.com

Printed in U.S.A.

Books by Marie Ferrarella in Miniseries

MARIE FERRARELLA

This RITA® Award-winning author has written over one hundred and twenty books for Silhouette, some under the name Marie Nicole. Her romances are beloved by fans worldwide.

To
Patricia Smith,
who always knows how
to make me feel good

Chapter 1

"C'mon, say yes. You know you want to."

Patience Cavanaugh pushed her strawberry-blond hair out of her eyes and glanced up from the four-legged patient she was examining to the man who flirted with her.

Granted, there was a great deal to recommend him. Patrolman Josh Graham looked like every woman's dream come true. Handsome, blond, outgoing with a killer smile, Josh filled out his uniform quite well. The very sight of him by her side would undoubtedly guarantee her the envy of every woman within a five-mile radius.

If she were into that sort of thing, which she wasn't.

Besides, the uniform was the source of the problem and the reason why she was going to turn him down. Again.

Life for Patience was filled to overflowing with police personnel. From her brother, Patrick, to her two uncles right down to eight of her nine cousins. And even the ninth one, Janelle, was associated with law enforcement. Uncle Brian's daughter was currently an assistant district attorney with a very impressive track record.

Patience thought of her father. He'd been a policeman as well.

And he had died in the line of duty.

Unlike the rest of the family, Michael Cavanaugh's work had turned him into a bitter man. Looking back on her childhood, she could hardly remember a day when there hadn't been some kind of unrest and turmoil within their small household. The job made him a hard man to live with. Night after night, she'd watch her mother hold her breath, waiting for her father to come through the door. Saw the tense interaction between her parents almost from the moment he walked in. Felt, along with her older brother who tried to take the brunt of it, the fallout of her father's mounting frustration. Frustration that encompassed what he saw on the job as well as his own performance, but that she was to learn about later. What she knew firsthand was that he didn't leave his work at the precinct. It gave him nightmares when he was asleep.

In a way, his work had haunted all of them.

Even before her father's sudden death fifteen years ago, she'd made a vow to herself that when she finally decided to get serious about someone, that someone would *not* be associated with the police department. The best way to stick to that silent promise was not to get involved with a cop in the first place. Socially.

Professionally was another matter. As a vet running her own animal clinic, she treated the whole of the Aurora Police Department's K-9 squad, making sure the force of five German shepherds was up on their shots as well as treating them for any injuries sustained on the job or off.

Which brought her back around to Josh Graham. He had started with the K-9 squad about eighteen months ago. He'd begun his campaign to get her to go out with him around the same time. She treated his persistent pursuit with the humor that was second nature to her as well as her shield. Josh took it all in stride, but he never quite gave up, either.

She went back to examining the dog's ears. "You know my rules about that, Josh."

"Right." Josh moved in a little closer to the examination table—and her. "Those would be your rules of engagement." She had delineated them with tact and force the one time when she perceived that he was seriously asking her out instead of merely flirting with her. He grinned broadly at her. ''Haven't you heard? Rules are made to be broken.''

With swift, sure movements, she worked her fingers around the animal's back and hind quarters, checking for any new lumps. Usually, they represented fatty deposits that eventually disappeared, but she liked staying on top of everything.

She spared Josh a look. ''Funny philosophy, coming from a cop.''

The grin never dimmed. ''It's because I am a cop that I know just when they need to be adhered to and when they need to be broken.'' He moved as she did, slowly shadowing her path around the examination table. ''Now, your rules are fine when it comes to other cops, like say Coltrane over there.'' Emphasizing his point, he nodded at the door as another patrolman, Braden Coltrane entered with his four-footed partner, King. ''Word is that the reason he's partnered with one of the dogs is because no two-footed cop could put up with him.'' She was finished feeling her way around the dog's fur and Josh made it a point to be right in front of her again. ''But me, well, your rule really shouldn't apply to me.''

Humor curved her mouth. They both knew she wasn't going to say yes. And they both knew he was going to push, just a little. It was a game at this point, and diverting. ''And why's that?''

"Because we're soul mates, Patience. I can feel it." He placed his hand over his heart.

Patience turned her attention to checking Gonzo's teeth and gums. The former were turning a bit yellow. She was going to have to step up the cleaning schedule, she thought. "Well, I can't."

He cocked his head appealingly. "You would if you went out with me."

She spared him a glance, suppressing the sigh. Another woman, she knew, would probably have been worn down by now. But another woman hadn't held her comatose father's hand in the hospital, praying that he wouldn't slip away; that there would still be a chance for them to find a better footing. To finally *be* a real father and daughter instead of what they'd been: two hollowed-out shells with appropriate labels affixed to them. She'd needed more from him, wanted more. Surly or not, he'd been her father and she hadn't wanted to lose him to a gunman's bullet.

But she had. And no more restitutions were ever made. It made her feel cheated and angry. And guilty because she'd been relieved that the tension her father generated in their home was finally gone. The angry man who should have never been a cop was no more. She missed the idea of him, if not the man himself.

A small smile lifted the corners of her mouth.

"I'd just rather stick to the rules right now, Josh, if you don't mind."

"'Right now,'" he repeated. "Which means you might not later."

She supposed this was what was meant by a never-say-die attitude. "Which means I'm being polite." She picked up the dog's chart and made the proper notations. She was aware that both dog and master were studying her every move.

"I'm not giving up, you know," Josh told her the moment she laid down the chart.

Patience sighed. "Yes, I know, but you are wasting your time. Really. I'm flattered, Josh, but I'm also serious."

"We'll see," was all he said, flashing her a grin that he'd used to melt kneecaps at forty paces.

She merely laughed and shook her head. "Gonzo's ready to go," she told him. "He's fine and fit for duty." Because the dog nudged her, she petted the animal and was rewarded with a big, sloppy kiss. Delighted, Patience ruffled the dog's fur.

"Never thought I'd envy a mutt. Down, Gonzo." The dog obediently jumped down.

She patted the animal's head. "On behalf of Gonzo, I take offense at that."

Josh never missed a beat. "You could plead his case over dinner."

She shook her head, laughing. "Go." She fairly

pushed Josh out of the room and into the hall. "You have a beat to patrol."

With that she looked out into the waiting room. It was early, before the official start of her day. Her clinic was open from eight until five, but she made exceptions for the police department, having them bring in the canines before office hours so that they didn't have to spend any time in her waiting room.

She made exceptions for any emergency that might come up, as well. Like people, animals didn't always come down with something during pre-scribed business hours. More than once she'd been on the receiving end of a frantic call that came to her in the middle of the night. Never once had she turned down a sick animal.

Which was how Walter Payne had come into her life. The meek software technician had called her, beside himself over his prized cockatiel. The bird had become ill at two in the morning. She'd never asked what he was doing, keeping company with the bird at that hour. Looking back, she thought perhaps that had been her initial mistake.

Because Walter's effuse gratitude had turned into something more. The flower he'd claimed came from the bird swiftly became bouquets left on her doorstep. There were poems and candy, all of which she politely but firmly declined, saying that payment of his bill was all that was necessary. But it wasn't all that was necessary from his point of view. The visits, with and without the accompanying cockatiel, increased until she'd begun to feel as if she were being stalked.

Not that Walter ever really worried her. She'd felt that the man was harmless in his adulation. But she couldn't get a case her father had been investigation out of her mind. She'd been ten at the time and maybe that was why it had left such a chilling impression on her. There'd been a young woman who'd been repeatedly stalked by a man she'd hardly known. He'd wound up killing her.

Patience had tried to tell herself that Walter and the other woman's stalker were nothing alike. Walter was a sad little man who wouldn't hurt a fly, but she'd struggled against ghosts from the past and at times it wasn't easy not to give in to the fear. Just to play it safe, Patience had made sure that the group photograph of her entire family, all in dress uniform—save for her and Janelle—was prominently displayed where Walter could see it.

It was a silent warning and, evidently, he got it. His attentions faded. Which was a good thing because she'd been certain that her big brother, Patrick, was just inches away from nailing the computer enthusiast's skinny hide to the back door. She'd made the mistake of mentioning it to him in passing and he'd been ready to take her in to file a restraining order against Walter. It had taken a lot of talking on her part to make him give up the idea; she'd known Patrick had been thinking of the same case her father had had.

Shoving her hands into the deep pockets of her white lab coat, Patience stood in the waiting room doorway and looked at her only other K-9 patient for the day. The other three had come by yesterday.

"Brady, you're up next."

"Don't forget to give him his distemper shot," Josh cracked, nodding at Brady as he passed by the tall, solemn dark-haired man.

Gonzo and King remained oblivious to one another as if they were wearing blinders. Brady gave a slight nod of greeting in response. His mouth never curved in the slightest.

Brady followed Patience into the examination room. "Graham giving you a hard time?"

Not looking in her direction, Brady gave King the command to get on the examination table. The sleek three-year-old German shepherd glided on as effortlessly as if he were a mere ten-pound puppy instead of the one-hundred-and-twelve-pound dog that he actually was.

Patience raised a shoulder, letting it drop again dismissively. "He's just being Josh. Persistent," she added when Brady didn't say anything. Not that he would. In all the time that she'd known him, she'd found Brady to be just a little more talkative than a sphinx. "I just think it's hard for him to believe that any woman would turn him down."

Brady said nothing for a couple of seconds, letting her lay out her instruments and get to work. "And did you?"

"As always." It was no secret how she felt about dating policeman. Everyone knew. She smiled at Brady. "Like I told Josh, I have my rules."

"Otherwise you'd go out with him," Josh answered.

Since he'd actually volunteered a sentence, she thought for a moment. "Maybe."

There was no question that she did find Josh almost as charming as the patrolman found himself. He had an engaging personality and she saw him frequently enough, either for the dog's routine exams or whenever her uncle Andrew, the former police chief of Aurora, threw a party. Her uncle did that with a fair amount of regularity and he usually invited half the police force. Josh was among that half.

As was Brady, from what she'd heard, but the latter never turned up. Word was he preferred his own company to that of others.

She glanced at Brady before she turned her attention to the dog's examination. Josh and Brady were as different as night and day, beginning with their coloring. Brady had black hair to Josh's blond. The only thing the two men had in common beyond their uniforms was that they were both good-looking. While Josh was outgoing, Officer Braden Coltrane was quiet. If she wanted more than a single-syllable conversation with King's two-legged partner, she had to go in search of it herself, often dragging words up Brady's throat and out of his mouth.

Silence obviously didn't bother him. He seemed to enjoy it. Even his commands to his dog were usually silent, as opposed to Josh's verbal ones. Each man, she thought, gave the kind of commands he was most comfortable with.

Because cultivating a conversation with him required so much effort, Patience found she had to live up to her name whenever she dealt with Brady.

She began working the animal's thick coat, going slowly. "But there's no point in speculating about whether or not I'd go out with Josh because I do have my rules," she said over her shoulder at Brady. She kept her explanation simple. "There's no way I'm going to go through what my mother did, waiting for my husband to come home every night."

Brady laughed dryly. "There are worse things than that."

Patience was quick to jump on the offering, looking to expand it. "Such as?"

He shrugged carelessly, looking away. "Having him come home."

Patience looked up sharply.

The sentence hung in the air between them. Had he known her father? she wondered. Because of his family name more than anything else, there were rumors that Mike Cavanaugh had been a disgruntled, dissatisfied man. The Cavanaugh brother who couldn't measure up. Was Brady referring to that, to the hearsay?

Or was he talking about something more close to home? She, along with most of the force, she surmised, knew next to nothing about the man.

Brady said nothing more. She tried to coax more out. "What makes you say that?"

"Nothing."

The curtain had gone down again. No encores followed. Patience let a small sigh escape as she continued to examine King.

Stupid of him, letting that out, Brady thought. His mistake. But not one he was about to follow up on. He wasn't about to tell this petite, pretty woman that for one unguarded moment he was thinking of his own past. Of his own father.

The man he'd shot.

The event haunted him to this very day. Any way you looked at it, Brady thought, he was truly an unlikely candidate for the position he now held. On the right side of the law.

Originally from a town so small in the south of Georgia that it didn't exist on some of the less detailed maps, Braden Coltrane had been just barely seventeen years old when he'd shot and killed his abusive father. When he'd been forced to kill him to save his mother and sister.

As was his habit, Owen Coltrane had come home roaring drunk. And as was his habit, Owen had begun to take his mood out on his wife and daughter. Unable to stand the tension he was forced to endure day in, day out, Brady had been in his closet-size bedroom, which had once served as the walk-in pantry, packing. Preparing to leave home for good that very night. He'd stopped packing when he'd heard his sister's frantic screams.

Rushing out into the living area of their run-down house, he'd seen his father threaten his mother with the gun that he'd prized more than his family. Not thinking of anything but saving his mother, Brady had gotten in between his parents.

His mother had stepped back, screaming as he'd wrestled his father for control of the firearm. In the struggle, it discharged, mortally wounding his father in the chest.

He remembered feeling numbed then shaken as he'd watched the blood pool beneath his father's body. His father had already been dead when he hit the wooden floor, a startled, angry expression forever frozen on his face.

A trial followed and he'd been found not guilty due to extenuating circumstances. Everyone knew the kind of man Owen Coltrane had been: mean sober and meaner drunk. But despite the stares and whispers that never stopped—they'd followed him wherever he went—Brady had remained in town, working at whatever jobs he could find to try to earn a living. He'd had to provide for his sister and bereaved mother.

His mother, who had never stopped blaming him for what had happened, died less than two years after his father of what the local doctor had unscientifically called "a broken heart." To Brady's everlasting bewilderment and anger, his mother had pined away after his father and although Owen had abused her throughout their entire marriage, she'd been unable to find a way to live without him.

Which led Brady to the final conclusion that he just couldn't begin to understand relationships at all. He certainly had no role models to fall back on. His father had been a cruel, vindictive man, devoid of love. His mother had been a weak puppet who hadn't loved her children enough to protect them from her husband's wrath. Though he had begged his mother to leave his father and start a new life for herself and for them, she'd always turned a deaf ear on his pleas.

Less than a month after their mother's funeral, Brady's sister Laura married a marine and left town. At nineteen, with no responsibility left, he'd been free to do whatever he wanted.

And what he'd wanted was to get as far the hell away from memories of his childhood as he could.

He'd packed up and left Georgia right after Laura's wedding, taking only a few possessions and the burden of his past with him.

He'd knocked around a bit, moving clear across the country. Settling down, he'd decided to go to college at night to earn a degree in criminology, a subject that had always interested him. It took him less than three and a half years. When he put his mind to something, he didn't let anything get in his way.

Eventually he came to Aurora and joined the local police force. He did well with the work, but not with his partners. An affinity for animals had led him to apply for the K-9 squad when an opening became available. He'd always felt that animals were truer than people, being unable to engage in deceptions.

And now he and King had a bond he had never felt with another living creature. He'd lay down his life for the dog without a second thought.

Patience looked at Brady for a moment, wondering what was going on inside his head.

In a way, the patrolman reminded her a great deal of Patrick before his wife, Maggi, had come into his life. When they were growing up, Patrick had always borne the brunt of their father's displeasure, partially, Patience thought, because Patrick looked a great deal like their uncle Andrew, whose career had been so much more dynamic than their father's. Before he'd retired, Andrew Cavanaugh, the son of a beat cop, had advanced his way up to police chief of Aurora. And Uncle Brian, her father's younger brother, was the current chief of detectives.

Her father had always felt as if he were struggling beneath the shadows of both of his brothers. He'd never come into his own and had harbored a great deal of resentment toward both of them. The only place he could freely take out his anger was at home, on his family.

Had Brady gone through something like that?

For a fleeting moment, without knowing any of the circumstances, or even if she was right, Patience felt a kinship with him.

Maybe it was something in his eyes. A startling shade of blue, in unguarded moments they seemed incredibly sad to her.

"You know," she began, putting down her stethoscope, "in addition to being an incredible talker, I am also an incredible listener."

He knew where she was going with this. Once or twice before she'd tried to nudge him toward a conversation that involved something more private than how King was doing. He'd steered clear of it then, as well. He had no desire to share any of himself. He was what he was and had no need for human contact of any kind.

Inclining his head, he slipped King's leash around his neck. Brady had witnessed enough routine exams to know that this one was over. "Too bad you don't have anything to listen to."

Couldn't say she didn't try, Patience thought. But then, Coltrane was a hard nut to crack. And she knew when to back off. Picking up the dog's chart, she began making the necessary notations.

"Well, I'm available if you ever feel you have something to say."

"I won't," he assured her. Everything he felt remained inside. It was best that way. There had been a period when he'd thought of himself as a walking time bomb, but he had gotten that under control. His father's demise had done that.

King responded to the hand signal he gave the dog, leaping off the table and then standing almost at attention at his heel. "So, how's King?"

"Fitter than most people I know." Retiring her pen, she slipped it back into her pocket and flipped the chart closed. Patience paused to pet the dog. "Okay, boy, you're free to go." King looked to Brady for a command. Patience raised her eyes to the patrolman, as well. "I'll see you next month."

Brady made no reply, merely nodded. In another moment man and dog were out the door.

It was almost time to open her doors. She glanced at her calendar to see when her first appointment was due in. Not until nine. That meant she could allow herself a decent cup of coffee.

"That is one quiet man," she murmured to the

dog who followed her around like a faithful, furry
shadow. She'd rescued Tacoma, a mix of husky and
God only knew what else, when she'd come across
the stray, dirty, starving and bleeding on the side of
the road one night. She'd taken her to the clinic and
ministered to the dog, keeping vigil until she finally
pulled through. Tacoma had rewarded her the only
way she knew how, by permanently giving Patience
her heart.

She heard the bell over the door ring. That wasn't
her nine o'clock appointment and, most likely, it
wasn't her receptionist yet. Shirley never came in
early. Maybe Coltrane finally wanted to say something.

''Forget something?''

She turned around to see Brady in the doorway.
He was holding a single perfect pink rose in his
hand.

Chapter 2

"Brady?"

Patience cocked her head, as if that would some-how help her take in the image of Brady holding on to a large German shepherd with one hand and a delicate rose in the other. She'd never seen anything quite so incongruous in her life. He'd be the last man in the world she'd think would offer flowers of any kind, much less a single rose.

Just goes to show that one never really knows a person.

Her smile widened as she held out her hand.

Brady realized by the look on her face what she had to be thinking. That the flower was from him. But why would that even cross her mind? There was nothing between them other than a loose, nodding acquaintance that spanned the last two years. Maybe something could have happened between them were he someone else, were he not hollow inside with no hope of ever changing that condition.

But he wasn't someone else and he'd never given the gregarious veterinarian any reason to think that he was. Or that he thought of her as anything other than the police vet.

Even if, once in a while, he did.

There was no way for her to know that. No reason for her to entertain the thought that he would be the one to give her a flower.

But someone had given her this gift.

A feel of loss echoed inside him, although for the life of him he didn't know why.

Bemused, Patience crossed to him. A smile curved her lips as she looked up into his light blue eyes and took the rose out of his hand. For some people, words worked best, for others, it was actions.

Coltrane, she already knew, definitely fell into the latter category. He was nothing if not a man of action. The phrase "strong, silent type" had been created with him in mind. For a fleeting second, she forgot all about her rules.

"I'm touched."

"Then you know who left this?" he asked.

Something cold and clammy began to rear its

head within her when he asked the simple question. She struggled to hold back her fear. To blot out the grim photograph she'd glimpsed in the file her father had brought home with him. A photograph of a girl, about her own age now, who'd been stabbed by her stalker.

Damn it, Walter *knew* better this time. She took a deep breath, running her tongue along her dried lips. "You mean, it's not from you?"

For a second he found himself engaged by the flicker of her tongue moving along the outline of her mouth. It took him a moment to respond to her question. Brady shook his head. "No, I found it on your doorstep."

Patience's fingers loosened their grasp, and the rose fell to the floor.

Brady bent to pick it up. When he straightened again and looked at her face, he saw that all the color had drained out of it. Her complexion had turned a shade lighter.

Was she going to do that female thing and faint on him? "You all right?"

No, she thought, doing her best to rally behind anger rather than fear. She wasn't all right. Damn it, this was supposed to have all been behind her by now. Walter's eyes had all but bugged out when she'd told him that the nine police officers in dress blue were all related to her. She'd thought that was the end of it. And it had been.

Until now.

Patience had to remoisten her desert-dry lips. "You found this?" She nodded at the flower that was once more in his hand. This time she made no move to take it from him.

"Yes. On your doorstep." He'd already told her that. Brady watched her closely.

"Just like the last time," she murmured the words to herself. Why couldn't she stop the chill that slid up and down her spine.

"What last time?" The question came at her sharply, like fighter pilots on the attack.

She stared at him. For a second she hadn't realized that she'd said anything out loud. And then she shook her head, dismissing her words. Not wanting to open the door any further into the past than she'd already opened it. "Nothing."

Brady scowled. The hell it was nothing. People didn't turn white over nothing.

"What last time?" he repeated. The question bordered on a demand.

She tried to smile and only partially succeeded. The knots in her stomach were stealing all her available air. "Is that your interrogation voice?" she asked him, trying to divert his attention. "Because if it is, it's pretty scary."

"Damn it, Doc, what last time?" And then he drew his own conclusion. "Someone been harassing you?"

Bingo. From her reaction, he'd say he'd hit the nail right on the head. It was there, in her eyes.

He could see it happening. Patience Cavanaugh was more than passingly pretty. She was vibrant and outgoing on top of that. But in this upside-down world, someone could mistake her friendly manner for something else, feel perhaps that she was being friendly beyond the call and go on to misinterpret her behavior as a sign of interest.

She blew out a breath and looked away. "Not lately," she told him evasively.

Get a grip, Patience. It's just a flower, not a scorpion. She laughed to herself. Right now, she would have preferred the scorpion. She knew how to deal with that.

Obsession—if that's what this was boiling down to—was something beyond her range. No, no, it wasn't obsession, it was just a man who was too obtuse to understand that she just wasn't interested. There was no reason to believe she'd wind up like Katie. Katie Alder, that had been her name. The dead girl. This would go away just like the last time, she promised herself.

Brady had no intention of letting this slide. "But previously?"

Best defense was a strong offense, wasn't that what Uncle Andrew always told them? With a toss of her head, she fixed her best, most confident smile to her lips.

"Really, Coltrane, there's no reason to get all official on me." She thought of their interaction over these past twenty-five months. "Although, I guess when you get down to it, that's all you ever are, isn't it? Official."

"This isn't about me, Doc, it's about you."

She squared her shoulders, deliberately avoiding looking at the flower he still held. "Right. And since it's about me, I'll handle it."

He raised a brow, pinning her with a look. "You weren't handling it a minute ago."

No, that had been an aberration. One she wasn't about to allow to happen again. She was stronger than that. "I'm better now."

He made a leap, bridging the gap from here to there and filling in the missing pieces. It wasn't hard. He'd handled more than one stalker case before he'd found a place for himself in narcotics. "You ever report it?"

She looked at Brady warily. She'd always sensed he was sharp, maybe even intuitive, but she didn't want to learn she was right at her own expense. "Report what?" she asked vaguely.

"The stalker."

Patience raised her chin defiantly. "What stalker?"

"The one who was after you," he snapped tersely. Nothing irked him more than people who wouldn't take help that was offered. Like his mother

who had refused to walk away from his father.
"Look," Brady began more evenly this time, "no-body turns that shade of white when they see a stu-pid rose left on their doorstep unless there's some-thing else going on. Now if you don't want to talk to me, fine, but you've got a boatload of police per-sonnel in your life. Talk to one of them."

Because she was a Cavanaugh, even though she considered herself the mildest one of the group, she inherently resented being dictated to. "How do you know I haven't?"

He looked at her knowingly. "Just because I don't get along with people doesn't mean I can't read them." Brady gave her a look just before he turned to leave. "Have it your way. Looks like I'm not the only one who isn't communicative."

It was as if he'd read her mind.

Patience blew out another breath, irritated. Re-lenting. The man was right, she supposed. And it was better to say something to him than to Patrick or the others. Especially Patrick. She knew without asking that the law took on a whole different hue when someone her older brother cared about was being threatened.

"His name's Walter," she finally said, addressing her words to the back of Brady's head.

Stopping just short of the door, Brady turned around. He stood waiting, not saying a word.

Okay, Patience thought, she might as well tell him

a little more. "Walter Payne," she elaborated. "I saved his cockatiel and he was grateful. Very grateful. He was also kind of lonely," she added after a moment. "I tried to encourage him to go out, to get out of his shell." She'd even gone so far as to suggest arranging a blind date for him. But although eager to please her, Walter hadn't followed up on her suggestion. "Maybe I was too successful."

"So he started harassing you?" He had his answer as soon as he saw the woman pale.

Harassment and stalking were such ugly words. She told herself that it was more like enduring a schoolboy crush from a forty-five-year-old man. She couldn't handle it any other way. "He brought me flowers, said it was from Mitzi."

"Mitzi?"

"His cockatiel. At first it was just one, like that." She nodded at the rose. "And then it was a bouquet. There was candy and a few poems, as well." Those had followed in quick succession. Crowding her. "I just thought he was being overly grateful. The cockatiel meant a great deal to him."

Brady tried to read between the lines to pick up on what the veterinarian wasn't saying. "You told him to stop?"

"In a way," she allowed. "I said that it wasn't really proper, that I couldn't accept gifts for doing my job."

Why did he have to drag the words out of her? he wondered impatiently. "And?"

Patience shrugged, blocking the edgy frustration that pushed its way forward. "He kept leaving them anyway."

He knew that these things almost always escalated unless there was forceful police intervention. "What made him finally stop?"

"I put out a formal photograph of my family in dress blues. Made sure he saw it." Patience nodded at the far wall.

There, hung in prominent display was a group photograph he'd seen more than once on his visits to her office. He looked at it with fresh eyes. The last time he'd seen that much blue was at a patrolman's funeral. He had to say it was impressive.

Patience allowed a small smile to surface. "I guess that put the fear of God into him. Or at least the fear of the Cavanaughs." Her smile widened a little. "Walter hasn't sent a poem or a single flower in the last six months. And he hasn't been by."

Brady looked down at the rose. King eyed it, as well. "Until now."

She nodded, suppressing a sigh. "Until now," she echoed.

If this was the resurgence of the stalker, she was being entirely too blasé about it. "You should report this, you know."

Calmer now, she thought of the mousy little man,

of the stunned expression on his face when she'd made reference to her family and had shown him the photograph. She'd overreacted, she told herself, because of Katie. But this was different and she didn't want to stir things up. "He's harmless."

In Brady's book, no one was harmless in the absolute sense. Everyone had a button that could be pressed, setting them off. "Every killer was once thought of as harmless."

She looked at him for a long moment. "You're trying to scare me."

"Damn straight I am. I've seen enough things in my life to know when a woman should be scared, Doc."

She'd been around members of the police department all of her life. Beyond her father, she couldn't recall any of them being as world-weary as Coltrane appeared to be. Not even Patrick. "God, you sound as if you're a hundred years old."

"Some nights, I am," he told her matter-of-factly. "So, you want me to take a statement?"

"No, that's all right. If I get really worried about Walter, like you said, I've got my own boatload of police personnel to turn to."

It wasn't difficult to read between the lines. "But you won't."

Patience didn't feel comfortable, being read so effortlessly by a man she couldn't begin to read herself. Rather than get into it, she gave him her reasons—or, at least, the primary one. "I don't want to upset them unnecessarily."

"How about necessarily?"

"Walter's harmless," she insisted. It felt odd, championing a man she wished, deep down, had never crossed her path. "He thinks he's just pursuing me, like in the old-fashioned sense. Courting," she added, fishing for the right word. Walter Payne always made her think of someone straight out of the fifties, when things had been simpler and persistence paid off. "He stopped once. If I ignore him, he'll stop again."

"And if he won't?" Brady challenged. King barked, as if to back him up.

Tacoma moved closer to her mistress, offering her protection. She absently ran her hand over the dog's head, scratching Tacoma behind the ears as she spoke, trying to keep the mental image of Katie's photograph at bay. "Then I'll deal with it. I have a number of people to turn to."

Damn but she was one stubborn woman. One could see it in the set of her mouth, in her eyes.

But before he could say anything further to her, the bell above the door jangled and a woman came in, struggling with a battered cat carrier. The occupant of the carrier paced within the small space.

"I know I don't have an appointment, Dr. Cavanaugh, but Gracie's been hacking all night and I'm worried sick." The statement came out like an

extraordinarily long single word, each letter breath-
lessly woven to the one before and the one after.

Feeling the dog stiffen beside him, Brady looked
down at his companion. The fur on King's back was
standing up as he stared intently at the carrier. Had
he not been as well trained as he was, Brady was
sure the animal would have gone after the cat, carrier or no carrier. The cat obviously sensed it, too.
Hissing noises began to emerge from the carrier.

In contrast to King, Patience's dog seemed bored
and trotted over to the far corner to catch a nap
beneath the rays of the early morning sun.

Taking a firm hold of King's leash, Brady spared
Patience one last look.

"Report it," he told her much in the same voice
that he used on King when he verbalized his commands.

"I'll handle it," Patience repeated firmly. She
turned her attention to the frantic older woman.
Work was the best thing for her right now. "Right
this way, Mrs. Mahoney. As it happens, my first
patient of the day isn't here yet."

And neither was her receptionist, she added silently. But then, Shirley had a very loose concept of
time. Too bad. The young woman had a crush on
Brady that was evident to everyone but the man
himself. Shirley was going to regret not being here
a tad early this morning.

Patience turned to look back at Brady and mouthed, ''Thank you'' before she disappeared.

She could thank him all she wanted, Brady thought as he exited the clinic. In reality, he hadn't done anything. Doing something was up to her. He unlocked his car. The hell with it, this was her business, not his.

Holding the door open, he gave King a nod. The dog jumped into the back seat.

''Not our concern, boy,'' Brady said as he got behind the steering wheel.

He placed his key in the ignition. Glancing up into the rearview mirror, he could see King staring at him. Brady tried not to read anything into the intent brown eyes, but the dog seemed to be saying that he was wrong, that she was their concern. Because they knew her.

Brady sighed. King always had a way of setting him straight. But this time, the dog was wrong. Couldn't help someone who wouldn't help themselves. He'd learned that a long time ago.

It had been one hell of a long day from start to finish. A bad night's sleep didn't help matters. Not that he ever really got a good night's sleep. His sleep pattern would have sent any self-respecting hospital-affiliated sleep clinic into a tailspin. He amassed his sleep in snatches, never getting more than a couple hours at a clip, usually less. Each night turned into a patchwork quilt of sleep and wakefulness.

The trouble was that he couldn't shut off his mind, couldn't find peace even in repose. Half the time he dreamed of what he had experienced during the course of the day or, more than likely, during his earlier years.

He supposed, in comparison to that time period, anything he experienced now was a cakewalk, even if he did deal with the scum of the earth at times. At least he had the consolation of knowing that he was ridding the world of vermin, making it safer for people in Aurora, people like Patience Cavanaugh, to sleep at night.

Contributing to the restlessness he now felt was the fact that Dr. Patience Cavanaugh hadn't been off his mind for more than thirty minutes at a stretch. Usually less. He just wasn't comfortable about her lack of action with this stalker thing.

The first free minute he'd had, he'd deliberately investigated if any new stalker complaints had been filed today. They hadn't. Big surprise. Maybe she'd turned to someone in her family with the problem. No, he had a bead on her. For all her friendliness, all her vibrancy, Patience Cavanaugh was stubborn and independent like the rest of the Cavanaughs. That meant that she didn't relish appearing as if she were vulnerable, as if she couldn't take care of whatever was going on in her life all by herself.

"Still not our problem," he told the dog that went home with him every night.

King gave him the same penetrating look he'd given him that morning.

Brady sighed. Who the hell did he think he was fooling? "Yeah, right, we're police officers. That makes everything our problem."

Muttering something ripe and piercing under his breath, he started up the lovingly restored Mustang that served as his single private mode of transportation from the time he had left Georgia behind in his rearview mirror. The only original thing left of the cherry-red car was its outer shell. Everything beneath the hood was new, or at least had been replaced once if not twice. The vehicle was in prime running condition. He made sure to keep it that way. Working on cars helped soothe him whenever he felt particularly agitated.

Brady paused before pulling out of the lot. He knew he should go home, maybe tune up his engine to work the frustration out of his system.

Instead he turned his car in the opposite direction and headed back to the animal clinic.

"Yeah, yeah, I know, we're not going home. At least not yet." He glanced at the dog in the mirror. "Don't give me that look. She's a tax-paying citizen. Those are the ones we're supposed to protect, remember?" King's face remained impassive. "I just want to check up on her, make sure everything's all right. Something happens to her, the department's gotta find a new vet. Which means that you've got to get used to someone else poking at you. You want that?''

King continued to stare at him.

''I didn't think so.'' Brady took a sharp right. The open stretch of road in front of him invited him to go faster. He did.

Fifteen minutes later he eased his car to a stop, parking across the street from the animal clinic, which was attached to Patience's home. After tossing the dog a large treat, Brady looked out at the two-story building. Except for the one just above the front entrance, the lights within the clinic had long since been extinguished.

The lights inside her home, however, had not. She was home. Most likely alone.

Brady settled in.

Chapter 3

Patience pushed back the curtain.

There it was again.

The car parked directly across the street from her home had been sitting there for a while now. Ordinarily she might not have even noticed it, except that for once, there were no other cars parked along the street. The neighbor who had a hundred and one excuses to throw a party was off traveling in Europe somewhere. According to the neighborhood gossip, he wasn't due back for another three weeks.

Everyone else around her parked their cars either in the garage or in their driveway. Which made this particular vehicle stick out. Even if it hadn't been red, which it was.

Walter owned a beige sedan. Beige, like his personality. Had the man bought a new car?

Her palms felt damp. Why did anxiety always crowd in the moment sunlight left?

Her mind was working overtime. She had to stop doing this to herself. So there was a strange car parked across the street from her house, so what? There were a hundred reasons for it being there.

She could think of only one.

She'd noticed the parked vehicle as she'd walked by her family room window. Ten minutes later, she was drawn back to the window. And again. Each time she looked, she could feel something in her chest tighten just a little more.

Get a grip.

She worked the curtain fabric through her fingers, staring at the vehicle. Telling herself that memories of her father's case were making her overreact. Walter hadn't hurt her last time. Why would he this time? Patience didn't know for sure that the flower had come from Walter. But it had begun the last time with a single rose. Just because Walter had sent it, didn't mean that someone else couldn't send her a flower for a completely innocent reason.

There could be all sorts of explanations for that flower. It could have even come from a new real estate agent trying to make an impression. Realtors were always doing strange things like that, giving you pads, newsletters, flags. Why not roses?

Okay, so where was his flyer? Flying off somewhere? She watched a bunch of leaves chase each other at the curb where she'd swept them. Gusts of wind had been blowing all afternoon. Fall was settling in.

Stop it, Patience, you're making yourself crazy. Just wait and see what happens next.

That was what she'd told herself earlier this evening—just before she'd spotted the car. Patience chewed on her bottom lip. Did the car belong to Walter? She didn't know. No, she wasn't going to break down, wasn't going to be the spooked female, was *not* going to let her imagination run away with her. She could handle this. At the very least, she had to be sure if it was Walter or just a car someone had innocently parked near her house.

Summoning her courage, Patience looked out a third time. And saw the vague outline of a dog in the back seat. The relief she felt was massive. It wasn't Walter's car. Walter was terrified of dogs. Each time he had come into the clinic, he made sure to steer clear of any canine patients in the waiting area. He'd told her that he'd had a bad experience as a young boy that had scarred him for life.

Okay, not Walter. But, if not Walter, then who? A patient with an ''emergency''? It certainly wouldn't be the first time she'd seen a patient after her doors were closed.

She'd even gotten a couple of calls from frantic

pet owners in the middle of the night. The last one
had been less than a month ago, involving an encounter between a Great Dane and a pit bull that
had accidentally gotten loose in the residential area.
Jogging with her master, the Great Dane had been
no match for the smaller, more powerful animal. If
it hadn't been for a cruising patrol car, Patience had
no doubt that the Great Dane would have been
killed. As it was, she'd spent the better part of three
hours stitching up the poor victim.

Determined to get to the bottom of this, Patience
slipped on a sweater and went downstairs to the
front entrance of her house. The wind was picking
up again. Two weeks into fall and the weather had
decided to surrender to the season. Patience wrapped
her arms around herself as she crossed the street.
She missed summer already.

As she approached the vehicle, she saw the man
in the driver's seat look her way. Because of the
location of the streetlamp, his face was bathed in
shadow. She recognized the dog first. King. Which
meant that the man in the car had to be Coltrane.

But why?

She leaned down until she was level with the window and his face. He looked none too happy to see
her. "What are you doing here?"

He shrugged carelessly. "I was just making the
rounds."

The hell he was. She glanced at his vehicle, one

that, even in this light, she could tell had been lovingly handled and restored. She'd had no idea that
he was handy around cars. Only someone who was
handy could drive an automobile like this. It required a great deal of attention. "In a '78 Mustang?"

He looked mildly surprised that she could identify
not just the make and model, but the year, as well.
"You know cars?"

She laughed shortly. In this light, the car looked
a deep blood-red. Not exactly the most inconspicu-
ous color for a vehicle. "Most of my relatives are
male. I'd have to be deaf not to have picked up
something about cars over the years. And don't
change the subject. You're off duty." She ran her
hand lightly over the dog's head. "You both are,
unless the police chief has suddenly decided to relax
the uniform code. Besides, you're part of the narcotics division."

He'd never seen her outside of the clinic and
without her lab coat. She wore a pair of faded jeans
that adhered to her like a second skin, a white
T-shirt that just barely covered her midriff and a
cardigan that did nothing to hide her curves. For
once her red hair was loose, falling in waves around
her shoulders. She looked a great deal more femi-
nine and fragile this way. Something protective
stirred within him, growing larger.

"Haven't you heard about crime in the suburbs?"

She fixed him with a look that said she saw right through him. "Is that anything like lying in the suburbs?" Before he could say anything, she began, "Look, if you're here because of this morning—"

He looked at her with an attempt at innocence she found endearing. "This morning? What happened this morning?"

She made no effort to suppress her grin. Amusement shone in her eyes. "If being a policeman doesn't work out for you, Coltrane, promise me you don't try being an actor. There's no future in it for you. Trust me, you're awful at it." And then her grin softened into a smile. "I'm touched." She nodded toward the house. "Why don't you come inside for a cup of coffee?"

He reached for the key in his ignition. "I was just on my way home."

"Sure you were." Before he could start the car, Patience opened the rear door. Instantly, King came bounding out. His tail wagged so hard, had he been a smaller dog he might have succeeded in levitating himself off the ground. Laughing, she ran her hand along the animal's head. "Well, I'm happy to see you, too. Why don't you come on in and say hi to Tacoma? I've got this great extra soup bone I don't know what to do with." She began to lead the way, but King turned to look at his master. His expression seemed to implore Brady to come along. "Don't worry about him, King. I already asked him, but he doesn't want to come in. He likes sitting in cars in the dark. Let's go.''

Turning on her heel, she started to walk back to her house. After a moment's hesitation King followed her willingly.

She probably had treats in her pocket, Brady thought darkly. Patience was forever doling them out to the dogs she treated. Disgusted at being abandoned, he leaned out the window and called, ''That's bribery.''

She looked at him over her shoulder. Even at this distance, her expression looked purely impish to him. ''Yes, it is.''

With a sigh, Brady got out of his car and shut the door. He made no effort to catch up to the duo. Instead he followed behind the clearly smitten animal and the woman who had made him give up his evening routine.

Not that it was any great sacrifice on his part. Evenings for Brady meant heating up whatever he found in the refrigerator, then stretching out in front of the television set, tuned to some news channel so that he could stay informed.

Law enforcement had advanced a long way from making sure the town drunk was locked up for the night. It had even progressed beyond the thieves, the drug pushers, the murderers, kidnappers and rapists that were all a part of the modern world. Now there was an international threat to be on the alert for, as well.

It never seemed to stop.

However, tonight the world had gotten a great deal smaller again and his focus was concentrated on the woman walking into the house, adoringly followed by his four-footed partner.

Entering the house, he followed woman and beast into a kitchen that was both warm and cozy. Something out of a sitcom, he thought, because it certainly wasn't out of anything he'd ever experienced firsthand. He remembered hearing somewhere that the kitchen was the heart of the house. In his house, the kitchen had been where his father liked to do his drinking when he wasn't throwing back shots at the local bar.

Brady watched as King followed every move Patience made. He liked her hair down, he noted, instead of up and out of the way. He hadn't realized it was so long. The tresses moved with her like a strawberry-blond cloud.

He straddled a chair. "You know, he's not supposed to do that. Divide his loyalties that way." He gave King a dark look. "He's supposed to respond only to me."

Patience tossed the dog a treat out of her pocket. King stretched, catching the bone-shaped snack in midair. "Don't feel bad, I have this way with animals, I always have. That's why I became a vet when everyone else around me was cleaving to the Aurora Police Department.'' And then she smiled, which Brady found oddly unsettling. ''I promise I won't get between you two unless absolutely necessary.''

He gave her a penetrating look. ''And this was necessary.''

''Absolutely.'' Taking the coffeepot she always kept brewing, she poured Brady a cup, then filled her own. Just talking to Brady made her feel better. ''I didn't want your butt falling asleep because of me.''

''No part of me was going to fall asleep,'' he informed her tersely. When she reached for the sugar, he shook his head. He took his coffee the way he took his view of life: black.

''It would if you sat out there long enough.'' Reaching into the cupboard, she took down two small plates. ''Just how long were you planning on staying there?''

He tried not to notice how tight her body was when she stretched. ''Not long.''

She shook her head. Opening the drawer beneath the counter, she took out two forks and a long knife. ''Like I said, you just don't lie well. Look, Coltrane, I'm touched—''

''Most likely,'' he said in a disparaging manner, which made her think that he meant the term in the old-fashioned sense, as in touched in the head, ''but it's my job to protect the citizens of Aurora and last time I looked, you were among that number. Besides…'' He paused to take a sip of coffee. It was so strong, it jarred his teeth. He gave his silent seal of approval. ''Anything happens to you, the department has to find a new vet. King doesn't like adjusting to anyone new.''

She turned to look at him, a smile playing on her lips. ''Oh, King doesn't, does he?''

He could see exactly what she was saying. That she thought he was substituting King for himself. Obviously the woman didn't suffer from an inferiority complex. ''You know, I never realized it before, but you've got a smart mouth.''

''Lots of things you probably haven't realized about me, Officer Coltrane.'' She flashed him a very significant look. ''Lots of things I apparently didn't realize about you.''

He cut her off before she began to wax sentimental or something equally as unacceptable to him. He never knew what to do when confronted with either tears or gratitude. He usually wound up ignoring both. ''I think we should stop the conversation right here.''

Patience nodded, agreeable up to a point. ''Okay, what do you want to talk about?''

He felt like a mustang, cornered in a canyon with only one way out. The way he'd come. ''Who said I wanted to talk?''

For a second she stopped what she was doing and studied him. "Well, you don't want to just sit there like a department store mannequin, do you?"

No, he wanted to finish his coffee and leave, but he kept that to himself. For the moment. "What's wrong with that?"

She laughed again and the sound went right through him. "It's too quiet for one thing."

The last time it had been too quiet for him, he'd found himself, without warning, looking down the business end of a Smith and Wesson. Other than that, he took his silence where he could. "I never saw the need to litter the air with words."

She gave a careless shrug of her shoulder and reached for a handful of napkins. She shoved a thick wad into the napkin holder she was always forgetting to restock. "It's only littering if it's garbage. Something tells me you don't spout garbage."

"I don't 'spout' at all." He regretted the impulse to drive by her house tonight. Just went to show him that no good deed ever went unpunished.

"I guess that's what makes King such a perfect partner for you." She glanced over at the dog who was hunkered down in corner, focusing his attention on the soup bone she had given him. Tacoma was close by, enjoying a similar feast. Patience could feel Brady watching her every move. "You always study people so intently?"

"You're not even facing me," he protested.

"I don't have to be." She looked at him over her shoulder. "I can feel your eyes."

He drained his cup. There was nothing to keep him here. So why wasn't he getting to his feet? "That's just not possible."

Removing the lid from a cake she'd just baked less than a hour ago, Patience paused before cutting into it. "So how did I know you were watching me?"

"Deduction." It was the logical response. "You're the only thing here worth looking at."

Her mouth fell open before she could catch herself. Patience stared at him, not sure she'd heard what she thought she had. "Is that a compliment?"

Annoyance creased his brow. "That was just an observation. That's what a cop does, he makes observations."

She sighed, cutting two slices and placing them on the plates. Why did he sound so put off, so irritated whenever she tried to guide the conversation to a more personal path? Who was he beneath that bulletproof vest? There had to be a softer side to him, otherwise he wouldn't have been there tonight, outside her house.

She brought the plates over to the table. "You make it very hard to say thank-you, you know that?"

"There's no need to say thank-you." Brady

glared at the plate she placed in front of him. He nodded at it. "What's that?"

Patience sat and made herself comfortable. She pushed one fork toward him and took the other one for herself. "I call it cake."

"I know what it is. I meant, why are you putting it in front of me?"

"I'd just assumed that maybe you'd like some with your coffee." She saw that he'd finished his and rose again, going to the counter to get the pot. Holding it over his empty cup, she paused. "Unless a can of oil might be more to your preference."

He nodded at the pot, indicating that he wanted her to pour. "What kind of cake?"

"Good cake." She grinned as she set the coffee-pot down on the table and took her seat again. "Rum cake. I made it."

It smelled enticing. Almost as enticing as she did. The thought sneaked up on him from nowhere. He sent it back to the same place. "You bake?"

"Bake, cook, clean," she enumerated, flashing a bright smile. "I'm multitalented. I'm still having a little trouble clearing tall buildings in a single bound, but I'm working on it."

He shook his head. Half the time she made no sense at all. "What the hell are you talking about?"

"The 'Superman' intro." There was no light of recognition in his eyes. It was as if he'd grown up

on another planet. "Never watched classic TV pro-
grams from the fifties?"

There'd been no television set in his house when
he was growing up. No money even for a cheap set
because every available penny went into his father's
shot glass. He'd started school in Salvation Army
clothes. Books were a luxury, never mind a television set. If there was something that his father
wanted to see, he watched it on a set at the bar, the
rest of them be damned.

The woman hadn't stopped probing since the second he'd walked into her house. "Why?" he asked.

"For fun. Do I have to explain fun to you, Officer
Coltrane?"

He'd absently taken a bite of the cake and he had
to admit, the woman knew her way around ingre-
dients. He couldn't remember enjoying something
so much. As he'd gotten older, food became for
functioning only. But this had pleasure attached to
it.

Now if she'd only stop talking…

"There's no need for you to explain anything to
me, Doc."

Patience picked at her cake, her attention completely focused on the man in her kitchen. The more
she talked to him, the less she knew.

"I beg to differ. Since you've taken it upon yourself to act as my protector, I think it's my duty to

reciprocate by opening up a whole new world for you.''

He put down his fork. ''This isn't a joke, Doc. I'm here because you have a stalker.''

Her expression grew serious. She didn't want to dwell on this. What she wanted was just to make it all go away. She didn't like looking over her shoulder, being afraid.

''Had,'' she emphasized. ''Look, I've been giving this some thought. We don't even know that the rose is from Walter. Maybe one of my other pet owners wanted to say thank-you.''

''So where's the note?''

She shrugged. ''Maybe it got lost. Blew away. The wind's been pretty bad off and on today.''

Was she afraid? he wondered. Was that why she was so determined to ignore the possible seriousness of the situation? ''If someone wanted to say thank-you, why didn't they just say it?''

''I don't know.'' Why was he making it so difficult for her? ''Because they're shy. The point is, although I really do appreciate it, you don't have to go out of your way for me, Coltrane.'' And then her expression softened. ''Unless of course you felt like coming over and sharing a cup of coffee with me and this was just a handy excuse for you.''

He wondered if she knew that her vulnerability was getting to him. ''The coffee was your idea.''

''You're drinking it.'' She shook her head. It was

official—her brother was going to have to surrender the pigheaded crown because there was a new champion in town. "Does everything have to be a debate with you?"

"It wouldn't be if you didn't automatically jump in on the other side."

"Sorry, it's in my nature." Patience shrugged, willing to back off for now. "There were a lot of people I had to hold my own with." She thought of her brother and cousins. "You know how it is."

"No," he replied flatly, "I don't."

"No siblings?"

Finishing his cake, he pushed the plate aside. "I have a sister."

From his tone, she made a natural assumption. "But you're not close."

He and Laura had once been extremely close, the way two siblings involved in a dire situation could be. But now both wanted to forget the childhood that linked them to tragedy.

"We exchange Christmas cards." How was it that she'd managed to turn things around again? "Look, this isn't about me."

"No," Patience agreed cheerfully, "it's about me. And I'm curious about you. This is the first time I've seen you out of uniform and outside the clinic." And as such, she wanted to make the most of the opportunity. She'd been curious for a while now. Unlike the other K-9 cops who came to the clinic,

Brady volunteered nothing. "You never come to my uncle's parties."

He finished his second cup, then set it down. "I'm not much of a party person."

"Neither is my brother Patrick, but he shows up." She reached for the coffeepot, but Brady shook his head, placing his hand over the top of his cup. Patience withdrew her own hand from the pot. She nodded toward the cake, silently offering him another slice, but he turned that down, too. "Haven't you heard, Coltrane? Socializing is good for you."

"General rules don't usually apply to me."

A rebel. She'd known as much when she'd first seen him. There was something about the way he'd held himself, something about the way he'd walked that told her he preferred the road less taken.

Why did she find that so intriguing?

"I'm beginning to get that."

Brady rose from his chair. "Good."

No, Patience thought, rising to her own feet, not good at all.

Chapter 4

Brady glanced toward King. The canine was still in the corner, doing his best to polish off the soup bone she'd given him. King seemed to sense that his master was looking at him. The dog raised his head and eyed Brady. It appeared to Patience as if the two were really communicating.

The next moment the dog abandoned both the bone and Tacoma and came trotting over, however reluctantly, to Brady's side.

She couldn't resist petting King's head. The dog all but curved into her hand, showing her that, Brady's partner or not, he was very receptive to the affection she showed him.

"I'm impressed," Patience told Brady as she

stroked the dog's fur. The top of the dog's head came up past her waist. If she hadn't known that the animal was a purebred, she would have said he had a little Great Dane in him. He was large for a shepherd. "That's some rapport you two have. King seems to read your mind." She flashed a grin at Brady. "Which is more than the rest of us are able to do."

Seeing how impatient he was to be gone, Patience walked Brady to the front door. Tacoma followed in their wake like a silent Greek chorus, just waiting for an opening.

"You don't have to walk me," Brady told her. "I know where the door is."

"I know I don't have to, I want to," she emphasized, stopping at her door. "Not everything has to be just for pragmatic reasons, Coltrane. Sometimes people just do things to be polite." Why was he so afraid of being friends? He'd obviously thought enough of her safety to put himself out and play sentry. So why couldn't he just accept her friendship? "You stood guard at my door for who knows how long—"

He interrupted before she could take off on another verbal odyssey. "I sat in the car for maybe thirty-five minutes."

"Whatever." She waved a dismissive hand at his words. Facts weren't important here. Intent was. "I wasn't asking for an accounting, Officer." Temporarily stymied, she sighed and shook her head before she turned it up to his. "Don't you *ever* loosen up?"

"This *is* loose," he informed her tersely. And if he was suddenly wondering what it would be like to kiss this five-foot-four, nonstop talking machine, she didn't need to know about it. Hell, he didn't even want to know about it.

But the thought lingered just the same. As did the curiosity.

"It's loose only if you're a steel girder," she quipped. She cocked her head and wondered all sorts of things. In the two years that he had been bringing King into the clinic, she'd only learned his name, rank and serial number. With his air of secrecy, he would have made a hell of a soldier. "Are you involved, Coltrane?"

Of all the questions she could have asked, this one completely threw him. "What?"

"Are you involved?" Patience repeated. Maybe Coltrane was so removed from everything, he didn't understand what she was talking about. "Is there someone waiting for you to come home right now, standing by the window and wondering why you're late?" she elaborated after a beat.

"No."

She shook her head, as if she'd stumbled across the root of his problem. "There should be."

His life was just fine the way it was. No attachments, no complications. Streamline. "I thought you were a vet, not a psychiatrist." If he meant to make her back off by insulting her, the amused smile on her face told him that he'd missed his target.

"Hey, even vets get to observe human nature once in a while," she told him. "And no one should be lonely."

His eyes narrowed like thunder clouds before a summer storm. "Who says I'm lonely?"

I do. But he obviously didn't appreciate her telling him so. She backed away. For now. "Sorry." She held her hands up in surrender. "I guess I'm reading into things again."

He accepted the apology, but his tone was far from friendly. "It's a bad habit. You should stop."

As she opened the front door Patience struggled to keep a straight face. "I'll work on it."

The wind whipped its way through trees now, clearing out dead leaves that went showering out into the night air, performing a macabre dance as they scattered.

The evening felt chillier than it should have been.

Patience knew she should go back inside, but she stood where she was. Waiting for something. She didn't know what.

And then a gust of wind took the ends of her hair, sending the strands gliding along his face. Brady caught a light scent that wrapped itself around him, dragging him in. He felt his stomach tightening.

The sound of her soft laughter echoed in his head.

Patience brushed back her hair from his face as well as her own.

"Sorry about that," she murmured.

An unfathomable look crossed Brady's face.

Patience wasn't sure just what happened next. She liked to think that Brady made the first move.

Or that they made it together.

But in all likelihood, if she replayed the action in slow motion, she'd probably discover that she was the initiating party. Never considered quite as vibrant as Uncle Andrew's girls, Callie, Teri and Rayne, she still took the lead whenever she felt something should move forward.

She didn't know exactly where she thought this thing between them should go. Looking back later, she doubted that she'd actually thought at all. Reacted was more like it. Sometimes, instincts just took over.

Maybe she'd been a vet too long and her patients had rubbed off on her. She didn't know. All she knew was that one second she was removing strands of her hair that were in his face and the next, her mouth had made contact with his.

And what contact.

It was something akin to the space shuttle taking off after countless delays. Lift-off was perfect, accompanied by anticipation, tension and a vast number of internal explosions that manifested themselves all around the shuttle.

If she truly was the initiator, all she'd meant to do was to make simple contact. Just brush her lips against his.

Maybe press a little.

Again, it wasn't a conscious thought process. And after contact, a thought process was the first thing to go in the meltdown.

Rising on her toes, feeling his arms tighten around her, pulling her closer to him, Patience let herself fall into the kiss. Into an endless, spiraling abyss. She was free-falling through space and it was the most exciting, delicious experience she'd ever had.

Brady had no idea what had just happened. One moment, she was just standing there on her front step, the warm glow from the light inside bathing her face in seductive hues, making him feel things that he had no desire to feel. The next moment, life as he'd known it abruptly changed forever.

He was here as a cop, not as a man. But it was as a man that he was reacting. And when the wind conspired against him, suddenly gliding her hair against his skin, making all hell break out inside of him, he felt as if he was fighting a losing battle.

But curiosity and desire got the better of him. He gave in to the former, did his damnedest to reconstruct the latter—and kissed her.

There had been many missteps in his life.

At night he would lie awake at times and review

them, thinking how different the course of his existence might be if he had just done some things differently. Even one thing differently.

And now this could be added to the list. Because until he'd kissed her, he didn't know. Didn't know that this woman could break apart his carefully constructed fortress.

At the moment of contact she made his head spin and his blood heat. It only became more so. The more he kissed Patience, the more he knew he wanted to kiss her. The more he wanted to take her back inside, to her bedroom and to find a way to release all this pent-up tension he was feeling.

His body was hot against hers.

She could feel the heat, feel the desire. What was she doing? She was breaking her own first rule, her own cardinal rule. How could she have just forgotten all about that?

But pleasure had a way of outweighing guilt. And panic. She kissed him as if it were all that mattered in this world.

And then, suddenly, air rushed all around her. And the night made her cold again.

Brady had pulled back.

She pressed her lips together, savoring the taste she found there, telling herself she shouldn't. He was a cop for heaven's sake and she wasn't about to get involved with a cop. Not ever.

Very slowly, she let out a breath. It didn't help. She felt as if she was still trembling inside like some kind of vestal virgin.

Damn it, what was wrong with her? It wasn't as if she were some kind of novice. She did go out. Just not all that often. Most of the time, she preferred the company of her patients or her family to a single, quite often awkward, one-on-one with a man.

Patience cleared her throat before finally venturing to put her confusion into words. "What do you call that?"

"A mistake." He took another step back from her and toward his car. Standing behind him, King danced away. The look on her face was sheer disappointment. Because of the kiss or what he'd said? "I'm sorry."

The words echoed in her head. He was sorry. He thought this was a mistake. Something twisted inside of her and she became aware of pain. "Was it that bad?"

"No," he told her honestly, "it was that good."

She knew he was complicated, but this made no sense. "Then why are you sorry?"

"I had no business kissing you."

"I think business is the last thing either one of us had on our minds."

She was wrong there, Brady thought. He'd meant business. It was only by exercising the extreme control he'd learned over the years that he'd kept from giving in to his feelings. What he wanted to continue feeling.

That he felt anything at all was something he wasn't about to analyze yet.

Or maybe ever.

He'd always thought of himself as not just part of the walking wounded, but of the walking dead. Life within his parents' house and the subsequent shooting had deadened everything inside him, except for maybe a sense of duty toward his mother and his sister. But his mother had died and his sister had gotten married. There was no one for him to take care of. No reason to feel responsible or protective any longer.

Once that was gone, he supposed that he had begun to search for something that might restore even that little bit inside of him. That one spark of sensation that had been left in the wake of his father's death.

But this kiss had punched a hole into the metal sheeting around his soul. It had showed him a glimmer of a rainbow he hadn't had any idea even existed within him.

Maybe he was just too tired. Maybe that was why he thought he felt something when there was actually nothing to feel.

He was too confused to sort out his feelings tonight. He looked toward his vehicle, still parked across the street.

"I've got to go."

Patience nodded. It was better this way. She wasn't prepared for what her body seemed to want. At least Coltrane had the good sense to back away. If he'd taken the lead, drawn her back inside and shut the door behind them, she didn't know if she would have been able to put a stop to what she knew in her heart would follow.

Rather than see him down the two steps, she retreated to the shelter of the doorway. "Thanks for stopping by."

He paused for a moment, then nodded toward the door. "Don't forget to lock up."

She laughed. Her brother and Coltrane definitely had things in common. "Now you sound like Patrick."

There wasn't even a glimmer of a smile on his lips. "Then you should listen to him."

Because he sounded so serious, Patience couldn't resist teasing him. She saluted. "Good night." She eased the door closed, then waited a beat.

"The lock," she heard him growl from the other side of the door.

She'd had a feeling he wouldn't leave until he heard the lock go into place. Patience laughed to herself and then flipped it. Listening, she heard the sound of his footsteps echoing into the night.

Patience leaned against the door, running her fingertips over her lips. She could almost still feel him there. The very thought made her heart start to hammer again.

Wasn't this a fine mess?

"So," she murmured to the dog who stood beside her and looked up into her face, "what are we going to do about this?"

Tacoma's answer was to retreat to the kitchen. Not only was her soup bone still there but the one that King had been gnawing on was there, as well.

She could just about make out what Tacoma was doing from where she stood. "Food." Patience shook her head. "Nope, that's not going to help here."

She wasn't sure if anything would.

The next moment Patience stubbornly told herself she was making something out of nothing. Coltrane had kissed her. Or maybe she'd kissed him. In any event, they'd kissed one another and although the fireworks she felt rivaled the ones at Disneyland on the Fourth of July, she doubted if the officer had felt the same.

Men never felt the same.

And so, being Brady, he would probably just shrug it off as an incident, nothing more. Certainly not something to lose sleep over.

The way she probably would.

Patience frowned to herself. There was absolutely

no point in her agonizing over something that had no life of its own.

"Maybe you're right after all," she told Tacoma as she walked into the kitchen behind the dog. "Maybe food is the answer."

She headed to the refrigerator. There was half a carton of ice cream in the freezer that could stand revisiting.

His eyes became narrow slits.

The anger inside his chest mounted in direct contrast, growing to huge proportions.

Threatening to explode.

She'd lied to him.

The little bitch was just like all the others. He'd believed her and she'd lied.

He dug his fingers into his hands. Blunt, jagged, nails pressed against his flesh, creating red crescents. One began to bleed. He took no notice. All his attention, all his energy was focused on the house in the center of the block.

Cursing under his breath, he retreated into the shadows again, the way he always did when he watched her. Watched Patience.

And he'd been here, cloaked in darkness, watching as she'd kissed that bastard. That cop. It should have been him on her doorstep, not Coltrane. He should have been the one to taste her mouth, to feel her body molding into his. It was his right, damn it. He'd earned it. He'd been patient.

Patient with Patience.

His mouth curved cynically. There was no humor there. Only frustration, only anger.

He'd waited, setting the stage, anticipating the moment.

And someone else had gotten to experience it.

He felt so angry, so betrayed, he wanted to rip something apart. Anger raged within him like a volley of artillery fire. He closed his eyes, clenched his hands and struggled to regain control over himself.

Maybe she didn't realize what she was doing. Maybe that cop had taken advantage of her. Smug, distant Coltrane wasn't fooling anyone. He was just waiting to pounce on her.

Well, he couldn't.

Patience belonged to him.

And someday soon, she was going to know it. And then he'd have everything he wanted. Because he'd have her. And she would make restitution for this transgression. So it would never happen again.

He watched the cop pull away in his flashy car. Good, he was leaving.

Becoming bold again, he ventured out a little, away from the shelter of the shadows. He turned his face toward her house. Only the lights on the second floor remained. The second floor.

Where her bedroom was.

A warmth slithered over his body as he began to imagine what she would look like, stripping off her clothes one by one, slipping into bed.

Naked.

His breathing grew heavier.

There was no one to hear.

Brady glanced in his rearview mirror. Standing on the back seat, King paced back and forth between the two partially opened windows. This was how the dog acted when they were on the trail of smuggled narcotics and he had caught the scent.

Except that there were no narcotics here.

"What's the matter with you, boy? Settle down." For once, King took no heed of the command. He continued moving from side to side. Damn but he wished the animal could talk. At least King would have something worthwhile to say. His thoughts turned to Patience, to the dumb move he'd made minutes earlier.

Taking a corner, he heard a thud behind him. King has fallen off the seat. "Sorry about that, but if you'd settled down and sat, you wouldn't have fallen off the seat."

Why was the dog so agitated? he wondered. And then it hit him. King was probably feeding off his own agitation. There'd been more than one time when he felt as if the animal read his thoughts, reacted to his tension. Usually it took place in the field, but perhaps the dog was attuned to his personal life, as well.

Brady glanced in the rearview mirror. Warm brown eyes met his. He laughed, something he rarely did. ''Yeah, I know just how you feel. She get to you, too, boy? Or was it that pretty dog of hers that has you going?'' King barked in response. ''The soup bone, huh? Thought you'd hold out for something bigger than that, like a lifetime supply of treats.''

Again King barked.

''What's gotten into you tonight?'' he asked. ''You'd think we were tracking down a main artery of the Colombian cartel. You know what we both need? To get away from things. To just kick back and lie on the beach.''

King's response was to bark even more.

''Yeah, me neither. It would drive me nuts within an hour. I guess we weren't meant to relax.''

As if in total agreement, King stopped barking and finally settled down on the seat.

Chapter 5

"Didn't I just see the two of you yesterday morning?"

Patience's words were addressed to Josh as the policeman and his K-9 partner walked into the first exam room behind her. Technically, this was the beginning of her lunch hour, and she'd been stuck doing paperwork thanks to the fact that her receptionist had bolted the minute the big hand had met the little hand at twelve on the oversize clock. Shirley was lovable and good with animals, but no one was ever going to accuse the pixish young woman of being an overachiever.

Once Mrs. Chambers and her Siamese cat had crossed the threshold and were gone, Patience had

had every intention of locking the clinic door. She needed to grab a bite to eat in her own kitchen and more important than that, she needed a few minutes to herself. A few minutes to unwind.

She felt exhausted.

For the most part, sleep had been notably absent from her bedroom last night and this morning. Consuming the remainder of a half gallon of ice cream right before bedtime wasn't exactly conducive to a restful night's sleep, but then, she knew that wasn't the real culprit for her sleeplessness. Kissing Brady had been responsible for that.

Kissing the quiet, brooding man had undone every neatly tied ribbon within her. She was at loose ends now, without the slightest idea of how to get herself back on track again.

One couldn't unring a bell. And one certainly couldn't take back a kiss.

What the hell had she been thinking?

This is what came of acting on instinct rather than logic. Instinct was all well and good if you had four feet and fur, but it wasn't nearly enough for self-preservation and survival if you walked upright and harbored a heart.

When she'd come down into the clinic, she'd tried to bury herself in her work. She was hoping to push the whole thing from her mind through sheer volume of work, but as luck would have it, almost all of her regular patients were doing fine today. Her jam-packed morning had gotten a great deal roomier when two of her appointments canceled and one turned out to be a no-show altogether.

By all rights, she should have welcomed Josh and his faithful partner, but the sight of the former's uniform served to reinforce her own lack of common sense last night.

Josh looked surprised at her less-than-welcoming question. "Hey, not so loud," he cautioned, pretending to whisper out of Gonzo's earshot. "He might think you don't like seeing us."

She flushed. Lack of sleep was making her punchy. She would have never phrased it that way normally. "Sorry, I'm a little preoccupied." She opened the chart she'd brought in with her. "It's just that he was fine yesterday."

Josh's broad shoulders moved up and down in a careless shrug. "You know how it is with dogs. Kinda like with kids. Fine one minute, problem the next."

Amusement highlighted her eyes. "Interesting philosophy for a bachelor." She looked back at the canine. "And just what seems to be the problem?"

Making himself comfortable, Josh leaned a hip against the examination table as he crossed his arms in front of him. "I think he's got something in his ear." He nodded at the one that appeared to be at half-mast. "He keeps pawing at it and holding his ear down."

"So I see." Patience smiled at the dog as she patted the examination table. "Okay, Gonzo, hop up here and let's have a look."

The dog jumped up on the table in one fluid, graceful motion, like a gazelle. Patience turned to pick up the instrument that would allow her to look more deeply into the dog's ear.

Josh shifted slightly, watching her. She was aware of his moving in a tad closer. "Can I help?"

Patience paused as she looked up from the animal. "You mean, you want to look into Gonzo's ear for me?"

He shook his head. "No, I meant with whatever's preoccupying you."

She smiled, waving away the offer. The question was typical Josh. He seemed to always be so ready to help. Brady was, too, she reminded herself. He just wasn't very vocal about it.

Still, finding him sitting outside her house, keeping vigil had really startled her before she'd realized that it was him. The man could really stand to take a few people lessons from Josh, she decided. For that matter, the man could stand to take a few people lessons from his own dog, who was a lot friendlier than he was.

If he's so unfriendly, why did he kiss you? More important, why did you kiss him?

If she had answers to that, maybe she would have

been able to sleep last night. She realized that Josh still watched her, waiting for an answer.

"I'm not really preoccupied, I just didn't get enough sleep last night, that's all."

He looked mildly surprised. "I was up until late last night, too. If you were awake, you should have called me. We could have done something together."

Shifting to the other side, she examined Gonzo's good ear to make sure there wasn't a problem there, as well. "Josh, you know about my rule."

He looked at her for a long moment. "Just thought you might have decided to bend it a little for a friend, that's all."

She rested the instrument on the examination table. Was it just her guilty conscience at play, or did he know something? Had Brady said something to him?

The second the thought occurred to her, she discarded it. Brady wasn't the type to say anything to anyone. She'd be willing to bet her entire practice on that.

"Why would you think that?" More than likely, Josh was just being Josh. Hopeful. Still, she needed to hear it from him.

The patrolman shrugged as he gave her one of his most engaging grins. "Hey, people change their minds all the time."

Discreetly she blew out a breath, feeling a little better. "Yes, well, I won't. Not about this."

But you already have, a taunting voice inside her head whispered.

One transgression. Just one, she thought fiercely. And it wasn't going to happen again. Ever.

It couldn't.

Patience looked into Gonzo's left ear again. They weren't here to debate her rules of engagement or her infractions thereof. They were here to see why Gonzo was holding his ear at half-mast.

"I see the problem. Poor thing's got a little debris in there." Setting the instrument down, she gave Josh a reproving look. "Have you been letting him ride around with his head sticking out of the window again?"

Josh spread his hands wide in protest. "Hey, I can't stop him. He loves feeling the wind in his face."

"And in his ears. And yes, you can stop him. You can roll up the windows. Unless I missed something very vital in my studies, dogs do not have opposable thumbs, which means they can't roll down the windows themselves."

"They're electric," Josh pointed out.

"You can also lock them from your side."

He laughed, shaking his head. "Got an answer for everything, don't you?"

"I try." She made a notation in the chart, then

turned to look at Josh. "You got off lucky this time. It looks like only one ear's been affected." She gave Gonzo the sign to get down. The dog leaped from the table. "You stay here, I'm going to take Gonzo in the back and clean out his ear."

But as she started to go into the back, where she and the part-time assistants conducted lab tests, took X rays and performed the occasional surgery, Josh followed in her wake. When she gave him a quizzical look, he explained, "Maybe I can help. Sometimes he won't hold still."

In the eighteen months she'd been looking after the animal, he'd never given her any problems. "You'll hold still for me, won't you, Gonzo?"

The dog barked in response to her tone, then licked her hand.

Josh laughed and shook his head. "Got him eating right out of your hand, don't you?"

She dug into her pocket and threw a treat to the animal, making sure to pet him, as well. "Only because he's such a good dog."

The dog trotted beside her as Josh brought up the rear. The back of the clinic was brightly lit as sunlight streamed in through tall windows on either side of the room.

"Listen," Josh began, "about that other thing—"

She went to a metal cabinet and opened a drawer. "Other thing?"

"You know, what you're preoccupied about—"

Patience took out two small bottles. One was an ear wash, the other a salve. "I said that was just lack of sleep."

Josh backed out of her way as she crossed to the animal. "Well, something must have gotten you to that point."

Taking care to soothingly pet Gonzo, she then turned the dog's head and tilted it. The dog was surprisingly docile, considering what she was doing. It was as if Gonzo sensed that she was trying to help him. "Haven't you ever had sleepless nights?"

"Yeah, but that's because I'm usually thinking about something. Look, all I'm saying is that if you wanted to talk about it, I'm available." He raised his hands as if to ward off her anticipated protest. "Strictly platonic. Just as a friend."

Putting down the ear wash, she took what amounted to a long Q-tips and applied a little salve to the end of it. She proceeded to apply the salve to the inside of the dog's ear. Gonzo whined, but held still until she was finished.

"Thanks." She threw away the swab, then gave the dog another treat. "But this is something I need to handle myself."

Josh looked vindicated. "So there is something."

She flashed him a grin. "Don't try tripping me up with words, it's nothing, really." She stepped back. "Okay, Gonzo, you're a free dog."

The police dog jumped off the table and immediately started to shake his head, as if trying to get the remainder of the ear wash and salve out of his ear.

Patience replaced the cap on the second bottle. "He might need another application of both. I could send an ear wash kit and the salve home with you."

Josh made no move to accept either of the small blue bottles. "I'm sure that Gonzo would rather you do it. You've got the lighter touch."

"There's nothing to this, really. All it takes is practice."

He still shook his head at the offerings. "This gives us an excuse to drop by."

She thought of the times the patrolman had dropped by unannounced just as she was closing up, always using the excuse that he was on his way home and thought he could talk her into grabbing a cup of coffee after hours. "Like you've ever needed one before. Okay, bring Gonzo by in about three days, we'll take another look to see how he's doing."

"Sounds good to me." Josh paused in the reception area as she made a notation in the ledger she kept at the behest of the police department. "And I meant what I said before."

She spared him a look before finishing her entry. "About the platonic part?"

He shrugged, resigned. "If that's what it takes to

get you to open up, yeah. Just remember, I'm only a phone call away if you need a shoulder to lean on or a hand to hold.''

Shelving the ledger, she walked out with Josh. She was already struggling inside because of what she'd allowed herself to do with one policeman. She wasn't about to compound her mistake by turning toward another. Not when there was a chance that Josh was doing more than flirting with her, doing more than just offering to be a good friend.

Things had a way of happening and she wasn't about to get involved with a policeman.

The crisp breeze wafted in as she opened the outer door for Josh and Gonzo. It made her think of the adage about shutting the barn door after the horse had escaped.

The horse, she told herself, could always be re-captured and secured back in the barn. And that was just what she intended to do.

''I appreciate that, Josh.'' She looked at the dog. ''If Gonzo gets any worse, give me a call and bring him by again.''

He nodded, then pantomimed talking into a tele-phone as he left, mouthing, ''Call me.''

She laughed and closed the front door again.

''Hey, you've been busy while I was gone.''

The sound of Shirley's voice pulled Patience out of her small office. Unable to quell the restless feeling that continued to skate through her body even after Josh and Gonzo had gone, she'd decided to update her files, entering the latest data into her computer.

"How did you know?" she called, curious. Shirley wasn't particularly intuitive. When it came right down to it, the girl often missed signs that were right in front of her. And it wasn't as if she'd left Gonzo's file on the front desk. She'd taken it with her to her office. The dog had been her only visitor in the past hour.

Shirley laughed at some private joke. "Because I almost tripped over them."

"Them?"

The moment she walked out, Patience saw what Shirley referred to. Her dark-haired receptionist held a long, white box in her arms. She was looking at it longingly, the way Cinderella might have at her stepsisters as they'd sauntered off to Prince Charming's exclusive ball.

"This." Shirley raised the box for emphasis, though not without effort. "Unless you're ordering really long thermometers, my guess is that these are flowers." She set the box on the counter that separated the reception area from the exam rooms. Shirley looked at her expectantly when she made no move toward the box. "Aren't you going to open it?"

Harmless, it could be entirely harmless. The flowers could be from a patient, or maybe even Josh for seeing Gonzo on such short notice. Or maybe even someone in her family thought to—

No, her family knew better than to do this. Patrick had told them about Walter and the white roses, but only after she'd assured him that it was over. Uncle Andrew had given her a long, stern lecture about taking unnecessary chances and made her promise to call him if she thought things were starting up again.

It wasn't starting up again, was it?

Patience crossed to the counter, stubbornly telling herself she was overreacting. This could be nothing. *Was* nothing.

She took a deep breath and slid the red ribbon off. It fell to the floor.

Her fingers felt almost numb as she removed the lid. And looked down at two dozen roses. Plump, perfect, pink roses.

"Gosh, they're gorgeous," Shirley exclaimed. She'd hired Shirley a month after the entire Walter incident was over. The receptionist clearly didn't know what the sight of roses did to her. "Look." Digging into the box, she produced a small white envelope and held it up like a trophy. "There's a card."

Patience uttered a silent prayer that the note was signed by someone she knew. But when she removed the shell-white card embossed with the florist's logo from the envelope and read, "It won't be long before you're mine," her heart turned to lead in her chest.

"You've got a secret admirer," Shirley exclaimed gleefully. Then she sighed, "Of course you would, just look at you."

That's what it had been called once upon a time. A secret admirer. And she might have even given the person the same label as Shirley had just given him—if she hadn't gone through what she had. Something that, Patrick had sternly informed her, could have turned very ugly.

But it hadn't. Walter had backed off.

Had something triggered him again?

She stared at the note. As much as she hated to admit it, she needed to do something about this before it got out of hand.

She stifled a shiver. Her flesh felt as if it was ready to creep off her body.

"Hey, are you okay?" Shirley peered into her face. Patience realized that for a minute she'd let her imagination get the better of her, shutting out everything else. "You don't look so good."

I don't feel so good, either. She forced a smile to her lips as she placed the card back into the box. "I have to make a phone call."

She began to retreat to her office, but Shirley didn't take the hint. Because Shirley was young and impetuous, the roses had set her imagination spinning. ''Do you know who sent these?'' she asked eagerly.

Patience looked at her over her shoulder. ''I have a pretty good hunch.''

Shirley's hazel eyes shone. She soaked up romance novels like a sponge, waiting for her own romance to materialize. ''Cool.''

Patience stopped just shy of her office, about to tell Shirley that, no, this wasn't cool. That this was most likely a stalker gearing up again. He hadn't hurt her the last time, but that was because he'd backed off. What if this time, he wouldn't? What if this time, he intended to gain the object of his obsession? Her.

Patience walked into her office and closed the door behind her. Her first instinct was to call Patrick.

But even as she began to hit the familiar numbers on the keypad, she dropped the receiver back into its cradle. She couldn't call Patrick and tell him about this. Patrick would only worry. And if he told anyone else in the family, then they'd be worried, as well. Not to mention turn overprotective.

In no time at all, she'd have her own armed guard posted at her side, watching her 24/7. Patience sighed. She couldn't handle that, either.

What she needed, she decided, struggling to remain rational, was someone on the outside, someone who wasn't personally involved, who wouldn't overreact. Someone who wouldn't let her family know.

Someone who could rival a clam.

An image of Brady popped into her mind.

The man was the closest thing to a clam she knew. She was pretty confident that her problem would remain a secret if she asked him to check this out. After all, the man only talked to his dog, and probably only after long intervals of silence at that.

Turning to her old-fashioned Rolodex, she flipped through the cards until she found Brady's number. Memorizing it, she punched in the numbers on her keypad.

The sound of his voice answering after five rings had an unexpected effect on her pulse. She told herself it was only because of the situation, nothing more. Last night had rattled her, the roses had rattled her more. She couldn't very well be expected to be calm.

But she was working on it.

There were a great many ways to begin the conversation. Small talk and chitchat, however, probably went over like a lead balloon when it came to Coltrane. He preferred going to the meat of the matter.

She served him meat. "Brady, he sent more roses."

The voice on the other end of the line was instantly alert. "When?"

"Just now. My receptionist found the box on the doorstep."

She didn't have to say anything more than that. The response was immediate. "I'll be right over."

She knew she should tell him that he needn't hurry. That tonight, after hours, would be soon enough. But she felt like a scared child because his words filled her with relief. "All right."

If pressed, she wouldn't have been able to explain why, but as she hung up, she felt calmer already.

"Patient in room one," Shirley called out.

Patience glanced at her watch. Right on schedule. Her afternoon was under way.

She went out to do what she knew she was good at.

Chapter 6

"She's in with a patient," the short, animated woman informed Brady when he entered the clinic less than fifteen minutes after the phone call. "But she's probably winding up. The dalmatian's been in there for about fifteen minutes." The brunette leaned over the counter to look down at his dog, grinning broadly at the animal, and even more broadly at him. "Something wrong with King?"

Brady shook his head, all the while aware that there was another man in the reception area. The man's fingers were lightly wrapped around a leash tethered to a drooling bulldog who looked as if he'd consumed more than one too many snacks from his master's plate. In an effort to forestall any trouble,

Brady gave King the command to heel. King duti-
fully ignored the bulldog. The latter seemed as if he
were chomping at the bit to sniff out the competition.

"Doc asked me to stop by," Brady told the young
woman whose name escaped him.

"For King?" the bouncy brunette asked.

"No," Brady replied patiently, eyeing the one
closed door in the back and willing Patience to appear.

"Then why…?" Since she didn't finish her question, Brady glanced in her direction and saw what
appeared to be a trace of disappointment on the
small, heart-shaped face. "Then you sent them to
her?"

Brady's eyes narrowed. Was she talking about the
roses? Before he could say anything in response, the
receptionist had rounded the counter and was on the
other side.

Cleaving to him, she lowered her voice as if she
were in the middle of some TV melodrama, striving
not to be overheard.

"They took her breath away when she saw them.
She could hardly talk." She sighed wistfully.
"They're absolutely beautiful. I wish someone
would send me roses like that." She looked at him
pointedly. The next second she seemed to rally and
was all but vibrating in her enthusiasm. "Must have
cost you a bundle."

"I didn't send them." Brady enunciated every syllable clearly. He didn't want to have to repeat himself.

"Oh." The hazel eyes widened as the fact that she'd apparently made a mistake sank in. She grinned as she began to backpedal. "Well. Okay. Um." A creak coming from the rear had her jerking her head in that direction. Her mouth quirked in a quick smile. "Here she is now." Not waiting for a comment, she hurried over to Patience. "Doctor, Officer Coltrane's here to see you about King."

Brady merely sighed and shook his head. The woman was definitely not up for employee of the year. Crossing to Patience, he lowered his head so that his mouth came close to her ear.

"Have you given any thought to getting a real receptionist instead of a Kewpie doll? Dish towels absorb more than she does."

Patience knew exactly what he meant. Shirley could be very trying. But she had a good heart and Patience felt protective of the younger woman. She felt a little bad for Shirley, seeing as how the woman had a crush on Brady. "She's good with animals."

He laughed shortly. "That's because her brain's the same size."

Though he'd kept his voice low, Patience glanced to see if Shirley had overheard. The receptionist watched them with a strange, unreadable expression on her face. Was she jealous? Did Shirley think that

Brady had sent the flowers? As if something like that would have ever crossed Brady's mind.

She couldn't help wondering if the man had ever been involved, then decided in the next instant that the answer to that was probably a resounding no. To be involved you had to give of yourself, at least a little, and she couldn't see Brady doing that. He was much too self-contained, too controlled.

Still, she reminded herself, he had come when she'd called. He could have put her off, or told her to call the police in officially, but he hadn't and right now, that was all that mattered.

"Why don't you follow me to the back?" Patience prompted. Her eye caught the disgruntled expression on the other occupant's face. It had "I was here first" written all over it. "I'll be with you in a few minutes, Mr. Matthews, I promise. This won't take long."

Matthews nodded, but grumbled something under his breath that had to do with police officers and undue privileges.

Patience saw that the comment didn't go unheard. A muscle in Brady's cheek twitched, but to his credit he gave no other indication that he'd heard the other man or was about to offer a retort.

"Sorry about that," Patience murmured.

Brady shrugged the apology away. "Don't worry about it." He didn't have to look behind him to know that King was following. "Where are the flowers?"

"Back here." Bypassing the exam rooms, she took him to her small office just off the operating area. The room barely had enough space for a desk and chair, much less the file cabinet and bookcase she'd managed to push in. Bringing another person in was a challenge. She glanced over her shoulder at Brady. "Tight squeeze."

That was putting it mildly, he thought. If he took a deep breath, he'd wind up brushing against her, something he really *didn't* want to do. "You could knock out a wall, make it bigger."

She'd thought about it, but the clinic already occupied a great deal of the first floor. "I didn't want to take space away from the examination rooms or the operating salon. I didn't need much space." Moving around to where the chair butted up against her desk to give him room, she gestured toward the long white box on her desk. "There it is."

"Was there a note?"

She nodded. A flicker of nerves washed over her. "It said 'It won't be long before you're mine.'"

He set his mouth hard. "Did you recognize it? Was it Payne's handwriting?"

She shook her head, frustration nibbling at her. "I'm not sure what his handwriting looks like. The poems and notes he'd send me always came off his printer."

That smacked of wanting everything uniform, controlled. Better to overestimate a suspect than to underestimate him. "Even with the flowers?" He found that highly unlikely, unless the man brought the cards with him when he bought the flowers.

She thought for a second. Only a few of the flowers had been accompanied by notes. "Those were printed, too. He has his own computer business so he's into all that."

He looked back at the rectangular box. "Is the card still inside?"

She nodded. Rather than open the box, she watched Brady take out a pair of rubber gloves from his pocket and slip them on. "I thought only detectives carried around rubber gloves. Aren't you and King in the narcotics detail?"

That was exactly why he carried gloves. "Sometimes I have to handle bags of cocaine or heroin," he told her matter-of-factly. "You don't want that getting on your skin, especially if you've got a nick or a cut."

Patience was barely aware of nodding in response. She was holding her breath as he took the lid off the box, bracing herself again. It was as if each time she looked at the flowers, she was reminded all over again that the world was not the place she wanted it to be, the place that her brother and cousins made safe just by their very presence. There was a nasty side to life, a nasty side that found them despite the best of precautions.

"Certainly isn't cheap," Brady observed matter-of-factly. Each rose was as plump and perfect as the last. Great care had been taken selecting them. By his count, there were two dozen.

"This must have set him back about a hundred dollars." Both hands in the box, he moved the long-stemmed flowers around gingerly.

He'd already taken out the envelope with the card and set it on the table. She didn't understand. "What are you looking for?"

He glanced at her. "Making sure your 'admirer' just sent flowers."

"What else would he have sent?"

He debated telling her, then decided that he'd rather she be safe than another statistic. Forewarned was forearmed.

"There was one case where the stalker sent a poisonous snake along with the flowers. When they caught him, he said that he felt if he couldn't have her, nobody could, and he made damn sure he got his way."

She'd put the lid back quickly, but was confident that she would have noticed if there had been any-thing alive in the box.

"No snake," she assured him. "Just flowers and a card."

But that was bad enough, she thought. Patience

sincerely doubted that she was ever going to be able to look at a rose without feeling an icy shiver go up and down her spine.

Satisfied that the only things in the box besides the roses were sprigs of baby's breath and silver tissue paper, he turned his attention to the card. Still wearing the gloves, he slipped the card out of the envelope and read it. The words matched the ones she'd already told him. He slipped the card back into the envelope. Dropping it into the box, he put the lid back in place.

"I'm going to take this down to the lab, have it dusted for prints."

"There'll be several sets. The florist's, mine. And Shirley brought the box into the clinic."

Shirley. That would be the animated woman in the outer office. "Might be a lot of people's prints on the box and envelope," he agreed. "But it's a start." And who knew, sometimes they actually got lucky.

"Um, Brady." He looked up at her. His eyes were edgy, stirring. She felt something inside of her responding. Just nerves. "I don't want this to get back to Patrick or the others."

"Strictly off the record," he assured her. "I've got a friend in forensics who can handle this discreetly." He saw the skeptical look that passed over Patience's face. "What?"

She shook her head, embarrassed. But he kept

looking at her, waiting. "It's nothing." And then she relented. "It's just that I can't seem to picture you with friends, that's all."

Brady eyed her for a long moment. He supposed he had that coming. It was no secret that he went out of his way to keep his distance from people in general. But sometimes, people got through anyway. Like Powell in forensics.

Like her.

He tried to tell himself there was no difference. "We're friends, aren't we?"

Brady's voice was devoid of emotion when he asked the question and she wondered for a second if he was being sarcastic or just incredibly dry, then decided that he was being neither.

"Yes," she acknowledged quietly, "we are." Friends was a nice, safe word that encompassed a wide terrain. Emotions were put into play with friends. That's all that was going on here, she insisted.

It only made her feel marginally better.

"Then you shouldn't have any trouble extending your imagination to my having more than just one friend," he concluded.

Brady started to pick up the box, then paused. Although she was trying to keep up a brave front, Patience seemed even more shaken this time around than she had when he'd inadvertently walked in with the rose he'd found on her doorstep.

Weighing his options, he made a decision. His assignment had just been brought to a satisfactory conclusion. He and King had just led several of the detectives in the narcotics division to a successful bust. Heroin dealers were using a school bus, of all things, to get their "product" from one place to another. King had led the detectives right to the stash, packed away beneath the floorboards.

"I can stick around for a while if you like," he offered.

It wasn't that she didn't want him to. The thought of having him around was infinitely comforting, but she just couldn't allow herself to surrender to her fears. It wasn't who she was.

"You're on duty and I don't have any narcotics for you to unearth." She glanced toward the operating salon. "Unless you're interested in confiscating some of the painkillers I have on hand—"

He never cracked a smile. "I can take some personal time."

The offer surprised her. But then, Coltrane had already surprised her by turning up last night. The man wasn't nearly as one-dimensional and aloof as he pretended.

She squared her shoulders, digging deep for her resolve. "No, that's all right. I've got a lot of patients to see today. And, besides, I have Tacoma for protection." Right now, the dog napped in the last exam room, but she knew all she had to do was call out the dog's name and she would be by her side in a shot. "She might not be as highly trained as King is—" she glanced toward the dog in the hallway "—but she won't let anything happen to me."

The look on Brady's face told her he was dubious about her faith, but he shrugged as he picked up the box. "You've got my number if you change your mind. I'll let you know about the roses."

Patience walked out of the room first. She had no desire to accidentally brush against Brady as they negotiated the doorway. She felt vulnerable enough as it was.

"I appreciate it. Really," she emphasized, sensing that if she went any further, she'd just make him uncomfortable. Brady Coltrane was obviously a reluctant champion, but she was grateful that she could turn to him. He'd find things out for her with a minimum of fuss. If she'd turned to Patrick, his first action would be to corner Walter and she still wasn't one hundred percent sure that it *was* Walter who was sending her the flowers.

Brady accepted her thanks with no comment. He went out into the front of the office with King close beside him. As he passed the receptionist, he heard the woman sigh. He gave no indication that he heard her. He had a feeling if he so much as looked in her direction, he would find himself detained indefinitely.

Brady went straight out the door.

Patience took a second to pull herself together, then walked into the reception area. She smiled broadly at the man sitting on the black sofa. ''I can see you now, Mr. Matthews.''

The man gained his feet and tugged on his dog's leash. The animal had fallen asleep.

'''Bout time,'' Matthews mumbled as he went to the first examination room.

It was quiet again. Funny how eerie she found that now.

She hadn't told Shirley anything about what was going on, even though the young woman had questioned her almost every hour on the hour about why Brady had walked off with her flowers.

''Did you two have an argument? Boy, I'd never stick with a guy who took back flowers.'' Her tone took a 180-degree turnabout. ''Although he is kinda cute. Now, if he was sending *me* flowers...''

For the most part, she let Shirley ramble on. The younger woman obviously had no great need for the truth. The more she talked, the more enamored she became with the scenario she was fabricating out of thin air. Very carefully, Shirley was edging her out as the recipient of Brady's affections.

The minute the last patient for the day had been seen and accounted for, Shirley had disappeared from the clinic like smoke. Tossing a hurried, ''See you tomorrow'' in her wake, the receptionist was gone.

Patience was quick to follow and lock the door behind her. Normally she left the front door open until she was ready to go up into her own house, but not today. Today she made sure that the lock was in place. She didn't want to leave herself more vulnerable than she was already feeling.

The phone rang and she nearly jumped out of her skin. The sound echoed and bounced within the empty clinic, mocking her. When she yanked the receiver up and exclaimed, ''Hello?'' she only heard a dial tone.

''Wrong number,'' she told herself as she dropped the receiver back into the cradle. ''It's just a wrong number. Damn it, Paysh, lighten up before you become a space cadet.''

As if to offer her comfort, Tacoma rubbed against her leg. She stroked the animal's head.

''Right, you're here to protect me,'' she murmured fondly, taking some comfort in the sound of her own voice. ''What could go wrong?''

It was dark outside and the dark always made her feel less than safe. Shadows harbored a multitude of tiny, pointy demons bent on torturing her mind. Her fear was a holdover from when she was very, very young.

Patience sighed as she flipped off a row of lights. What she needed was some hot tea. No, she decided more firmly, what she needed was not to let her imagination run off with her.

If this sudden rash of unwanted attention was coming from Walter, well, she'd been through this before. The man just needed a refresher course in leaving her alone.

And yet the tension refused to leave.

She didn't like being nervous. It reminded her too much of her childhood. Patrick and the others had always thought of her as the cheerful one, the one who had come through the experience of their less-than-storybook childhood unscathed.

But they were wrong. She hadn't.

She'd just maintain that outward, chipper facade to help bolster her mother and to help Patrick, as if being sunny and upbeat could somehow enable him to lighten the load he carried for all of them. She kept hoping her cheerfulness, however forced and unfounded, would rub off on him. Eventually her brother had found his answers and his haven in Maggi. Still, she felt that in her own small way, she'd done her damnedest to make life bearable for him and her mother.

She'd pretended to be carefree and unaffected for so long, she didn't know how else to behave. There were even times when she managed to fool herself into believing that she was the person she pretended to be. Happy, outgoing, secure.

But underneath it all was that frightened little girl

who cowered inside. The one who'd hidden in her room with her hands over her ears so as not to hear the sound of raised, ugly voices. And this resurgence of the stalker just brought it to the fore again.

Patience stifled a scream that swelled in her throat in response to the unexpected knock on the door. Trying to calm her nerves, she immediately reached for Tacoma's collar and slipped her fingers around it, as if tethering herself to the animal.

"We're closed," she called out.

"I know, that's why I'm here."

Patience felt her heart slam against her rib cage as the words registered half a beat before the voice did. Was she imagining it?

"Brady?"

This time, the voice from the other side of the door sounded more human. "Open the door, Doc. It's starting to rain and King smells like hell when he's wet."

A smile threatened to crack her face in two as she ran to the door and undid the locks.

Throwing the door open, Patience stepped back as the welcome sight of officer, dog and even rain came across the threshold as one.

A myriad of emotions swirled within her. More rain swept in and she came to, quickly shutting the door.

"Where did the rain come from?" she asked.

"The sky," he deadpanned. King shook himself off, sending a spray of raindrops in Tacoma's and

Patience's direction. "King, no!" he ordered, then looked at Patience. The bottom of her lab coat was covered with droplets. "Sorry about that."

"Don't be. Don't be sorry at all." She was fairly beaming as she said it.

Chapter 7

Tacoma sneezed and took a step back after attempting to inhale King's essence. Man and dog were leaving a trail of small puddles as they came into the center of the barren reception area.

Patience tried to remember the last time anyone had looked this good to her and couldn't. "What are you doing here?"

"Dripping." Brady rubbed his hand over his face in an effort to wipe off water. The downpour had been unexpected and sudden.

Patience laughed. "Besides that." Circumventing the counter, she crossed to the cabinets just off the operating salon. After taking out two towels from the lower cabinet, she offered one to Brady before

sinking to her knees and using the other to towel off
King. "Did you get anything back from the lab
yet?"

"Nothing definitive." She looked at him as he
ran the towel over his head. He looked boyish with
his hair going in all directions. Somehow, she knew
he wouldn't appreciate her making the observation.
"Like we already thought, there are several sets of
prints on the box—and two on the card. Yours and
an unknown party." As dry as he could make himself, he draped the towel over the back of the sofa.
"This Walter Payne, he's not a civil servant or anything, is he?"

She shook her head. "No, he runs his own business. Works out of his house."

He sighed. That meant, unless the man had been
arrested for something, his prints were not in the
system. "Didn't think it would be easy."

Finished toweling off King, she rose to her feet.
King nosed her pocket. Patience took out a treat and
tossed it to the dog. But her eyes were on Brady. "I
really appreciate this."

"There is no 'this' yet," he pointed out. "But
there will be."

She smiled, taking their damp towels and tossing
them in the hamper. "I had no idea you were an
optimist."

He didn't like having labels applied to him. "It's
not optimism, it's fact. Most stalkers tip their hand

early. They want to be near the object of their obsession.'' He saw her running her hands over her arms. ''Sorry. Didn't mean to scare you.''

She was going to have to get a better grip, Patience upbraided herself. It was just that the word ''obsession'' conjured up a host of awful feelings.

''You didn't,'' she told him cheerfully. ''I know all that.'' She paused and he didn't say anything. ''So, is that what you came by to tell me? That the lab evidence is inconclusive?''

He shrugged, not entirely comfortable with his decision, but less comfortable with leaving her by herself for the entire evening. He couldn't bring himself to dismiss the unguarded look of fear he'd seen on her face this afternoon. ''That and I thought I'd hang around for a while. In case.''

The phrase covered a vast myriad of scenarios. ''In case...'' she echoed. Now that he was here, she realized just how skittish she felt alone. Even with Tacoma. Having him here made her feel infinitely better. ''Why don't I send out for some dinner? If you're putting yourself out like this, the least I can do is feed you.''

Brady was about to argue, to say that he wasn't putting himself out, that this was all part of being a policeman, but he was already getting the feeling that arguing with Patience usually resulted in defeat. So he shrugged. ''Fine.''

''C'mon up into the house.'' Switching off the

light, she led the way to the back stairs that took her from the clinic into the main house. Once he and the dogs had crossed the threshold, she locked the connecting door and tried it once to make sure the lock had taken. "Any preferences?"

He looked at her. For a moment, a different answer threatened to materialize. He'd discovered a new preference last night. A preference for soft lips that tasted faintly of berries.

Brady roused himself before answering. "King likes egg rolls. Chicken," he added.

She laughed. "King and I have something in common, then." She ruffled the dog's fur, her eyes dancing. "Chinese it is."

How did she do that? he wondered, watching her as she walked to the telephone in the kitchen to place the order. How did she make her eyes dance like that? How did she manage to light up a room just by entering it?

He told himself that answers to those questions didn't concern him. Only the identity of her stalker did.

Dinner arrived in three large bags that managed to remain together only long enough for the wet delivery boy to transfer them into her hands. Since it was all casual, they ate in the living room, spreading out the seven containers on the coffee table.

Once they were seated on the floor and eating,

Patience tried to draw him out a little, determined to get to know this man who seemed so bent on remaining a closed book.

"Where are you from?" Emptying out the fried rice container, she divided what was left between their two plates.

The question, coming out of the blue and not following any given logical order, caught him off guard. "Here and there."

She proceeded to make short work of what was left on her plate. "Did either 'here' or 'there' involve the deep South?"

Suspicion entered his eyes as he raised them to hers. "Why?"

"Because you've got a slight accent. Not usually, but when you say some of your words, I can hear a drawl." He volunteered nothing and she shook her head. "You know, if we're supposed to be friends like you said, then friends know things about each other."

He considered her words for a minute, then resumed eating. "Maybe we should downgrade that to acquaintances."

Having traveled out on the limb, she wasn't ready to scoot back yet. "Hiding some deep, dark secret?" The look he gave her took her breath away. And fueled thoughts in her head. She had no idea why, but instantly thoughts of her own past—and Patrick's—rose in her mind.

"Sorry," she murmured, turning her attention back to her plate. She cut her egg roll in two, saving part of it for the dog that was eyeing her fork's every movement intently. "I didn't mean to pry."

"Yeah, you did."

She thought of the way Patrick had reacted, how hard it had been for him to finally come around, even years after their father's death. "You know, whatever happened, you're not defined by it."

Brady watched her for a long moment. Did she know? The incident and the trial had been written up in the local paper as well as several of the bigger ones, but he'd always assumed that the story hadn't gone outside the state. And what was in his file when he signed up with the police force was supposed to be strictly confidential. Had Patience found her way into his file because of her connections?

"What would you know about that?" he asked.

"A lot." Her voice became serious. "My dad was the Cavanaugh who didn't quite measure up." Brady looked at her sharply. "Uncle Andrew and Uncle Brian were damn near perfect. Great cops, wonderful fathers, even if the job kept them away from their families at times. My dad always felt inferior to them, like everything he did was always second or third best." If he'd only been satisfied with the love of his wife and children, rather than trying to outdo his brothers, things might have been different. For all of them. But there was no changing the past. ''That didn't sit well with him.''

. Thinking of his own life, Brady read between the lines. ''And he took it out on you?''

She had been the least singled out. For a second family loyalty warred with the feeling that she needed to reach Brady, to keep him from retreating further into himself, to the exclusion of the rest of the world. ''On everyone at home. He cheated on my mother, drank, lashed out a lot at Patrick.''

''And you?''

She lifted a shoulder in a half shrug. ''Sometimes. Mostly he ignored me because he was too busy venting against Patrick or my mother.'' If there'd been any love between her parents, it had been long gone by the time she'd been old enough to become aware of things. In its place there'd been fear and anger. ''He thought of her as second best, too.''

Brady didn't quite follow. ''Second best?''

She nodded, deliberately trying to keep the words at bay. She still ached for what her mother had gone through. ''I found out after he died that he had a thing for Aunt Rose—Uncle Andrew's wife.''

''Must have been hard on your mother.''

The simple comment, indicating that he was sensitive to what her mother had gone through, surprised Patience. ''Yes, it was.''

Brady thought of his sister, of how Laura had reacted to their father's mistreatment of their mother. She'd felt humiliated. "And you."

It hadn't been hard to see herself in her mother's place, to envision herself loving a man too much, letting him reign over her soul. That as much as anything had kept her from becoming serious about anything but her work. She shrugged.

"But it's over now."

He glanced at her knowingly. "Is it?"

She looked at him for a long moment. They were talking about him, not her, or at least they were supposed to be, she thought. "You tell me."

The silence slipped back around them, augmented by the sound of the dogs eating. And then he finally said, "Georgia."

"What?"

"I'm from Georgia," he said. There was almost a defiance in his voice. "Or was. I left ten years ago."

His words struck a familiar chord. Kindred spirits had a way of finding one another. She knew the signs. Had seen them in Patrick's eyes more than once. "Couldn't take it anymore," she said. It wasn't really a question. There was a time when she'd been afraid that Patrick would leave, but then their father had been shot and everything had changed.

Brady cracked open a fortune cookie. The fortune told him to lower his guard and let love in. Who the hell wrote these things? he wondered. He rolled the fortune up between his thumb and forefinger before discarding it on his plate. "Nothing left to take. My father was dead, so was my mother. Some marine married my sister. She left town when he got shipped out."

Brady probably thought he masked it well, but she detected just a hint of loneliness in his voice. She stifled the urge to reach out and touch his hand in mute comfort. He'd probably just jerk it away.

"No other family?" He shook his head. "So you came out here?"

The path had been far from straight. "Eventually."

"Right, first came 'here and there.'" She kept her curiosity about the locations to herself. "What made you want to become a cop?"

"To keep men from beating up on women."

That was the most telling remark of all, she thought. Except for once, her father hadn't hit her mother. The marks he'd left had been on her soul. "That's not narcotics," she pointed out.

"In some cases, that's the start."

"Your father's?" The question was out before she could stop it.

He'd already told her way more than he'd intended. He didn't like sharing himself, didn't like feeling exposed. "Maybe you should transfer from being the police vet to the police shrink."

''Sorry, I thought we were on a roll here.''

It was more of a case of her operating a steam-roller, he thought.

''You were, I wasn't.'' He looked at King, who was still patiently watching them eat. ''Speaking of rolls, any more egg rolls left?''

''Got some here I've been saving.'' She passed him the half she'd cut earlier. Brady in turn offered it to King. The piece was gone in less time than it took to pass the plate.

Patience knew she shouldn't question him further, no matter how much more she wanted to learn about him.

Brady stayed another hour, then prepared to leave.

''You sure you'll be all right?''

''I'll be fine. Thanks.'' She brushed her lips against his.

He caught himself before he could take her into his arms. He'd already gone too far this evening by letting her know bits and pieces about himself. Kissing her in this state was not a good idea.

''Lock your doors,'' he instructed, then left with King bringing up the rear.

She could lock her doors. The trouble was, she couldn't lock down her brain. Her thoughts about the evening, about Brady, replayed themselves through her mind. Brady, more than any threat of a stalker, kept her from getting a good night's sleep.

Curiosity nibbled away at her. Yes, he'd allowed her a glimpse into his life, but Brady'd left a great deal unsaid, things she wanted to know about the man who was her brooding protector.

By midmorning the next day Patience decided to do something about all the unanswered questions ricocheting in her brain. She took her questions to the one person who wouldn't be tempted to talk to anyone else in the family about her query.

She called Rayne, Uncle Andrew's youngest daughter.

The one-time hellion now had the distinction of being the youngest detective on the Aurora police force. Closing the door to her tiny office, Patience punched in her cousin's cell phone number.

Six rings went by before she heard anyone answer.

"Cavanaugh."

"Rayne, it's Patience."

"Talk fast, cousin." Rayne sounded breathless, as if she was hurrying somewhere. "I'm late."

So what else was new? Patience thought. Rayne's oldest brother, Shaw, liked to say that Rayne had been born several days past her due date and had been late ever since. It wasn't far from the truth, although lately, Rayne had been improving. A little.

"What do you know about Braden Coltrane?" Even as she asked, a sliver of guilt pricked at her conscience. "He's with the K-9 squad."

"I know who Coltrane is," Rayne told her. "And as for your question, not much." Interest peaked in her voice. "Why?"

"I just get vibes off him." She didn't know how else to put it.

"Vibes? What kind of vibes? This sounds interesting, Paysh."

Ever since her cousin had hooked up with Cole Garrison when the latter had returned to town to prove his younger brother innocent of a murder charge, Rayne had become a completely different woman. Her focus had changed, too. Where before she'd just storm-troop through life, she now took a vital interest in everything around her. Such as her cousin's romantic life.

Patience wanted to set Rayne straight. "He sounds like he might have had the kind of upbringing that Patrick and I had."

"Sorry, I don't know," Rayne confessed. Patience heard the sound of a car being started up. "But I can look into it for you."

For a moment Patience was tempted, but it felt too much like spying.

Or stalking.

This was a bad idea. Brady needed to tell her about his background himself, not have her find the information out by going behind his back. "Never mind. Thanks anyway."

"Hey, it's no trouble. I know someone in Human Resources—"

Patience laughed. It was no secret that Rayne had gotten around when she was younger. That included periodically running away. Half the force knew her on sight because they were always bringing her back to Uncle Andrew. "You know someone everywhere, Rayne. No, I shouldn't be prying."

"Okay." Rayne had always been a strong believer in privacy. But she was also a strong believer in satisfying curiosity. "Offer's open if you change your mind."

"Thanks, I'll remember that."

Rayne disconnected the call. Patience let the receiver drop back into its cradle. If she was going to find things out about Brady, it was going to be the old-fashioned way—by having him tell her.

She had the feeling that he'd almost told her something last night, then backed off, as if the subject wasn't to be handled. Had he been beaten as a child? Humiliated? Abused? Had he seen his own mother abused? She doubted if there was anything he could tell her that she couldn't relate to from her own past. But she wanted him to feel like he could talk to her. And that, she knew, was going to take time.

There were no flowers.

Each day, Patience held her breath, waiting. First

one day passed and then another, and no roses were left on her doorstep, no poems showed up in her mailbox, the way they had the last time Walter Payne had set his sights on her.

Each day she felt a little more confident.

She was beginning to think she was in the clear. Maybe whatever had prompted Walter to act had faded, an emotional blip he'd ridden out.

She said as much to Brady when he called the afternoon of the third day to check on her.

"All's clear on the western front," she kidded in response to his inquiry about the recurrence of any flowers or other signs of unwanted attention. "I think this was a momentary flare-up and he's thought better of it." For lack of a suspect, she'd decided to agree with Brady that the sender was most likely Walter.

"We'll see."

She heard the skepticism in his voice. Maybe it was childish, but she wanted him to say something reassuring, to tell her that it was over. "You're supposed to be more encouraging than that."

"I don't deal in encouragement." He sounded annoyed. "I deal in reality."

"Right." And the reality, she knew, was that she wasn't completely out of the woods yet. But she chose to think that she was. She wanted to celebrate. And to thank Brady for being there for her. She could have turned to Josh if she'd wanted to avoid her family, but somehow Brady made her feel safer. "Does dinner sound real enough for you?"

"Come again?"

"I thought you and King might want to stop by for dinner—unless you have other plans."

There was a long pause on the other end of the line. So long that she thought maybe he'd hung up. And then she heard him.

"No."

Again she waited, but there was no follow-up. Conversation with this man was definitely a challenge. "No, you can't come or no, you don't have other plans?"

"The latter."

She bit back a laugh. She didn't want him thinking she was laughing at him. "Good, then stop by. Tacoma is going through King withdrawals. She keeps looking at me when I close up the clinic at night, as if she's asking me why isn't King here."

"So this is about King."

Was that humor in his voice? Maybe the connection was fading. "Yeah, but you can come, too, Coltrane. We're friends, remember?"

"I thought we decided to downgrade that."

No, that was definitely humor there. My God, the man was human. "Don't remember any such decision being made. Look, I made a huge lasagna and I can't eat it by myself. I thought we might give King a new taste treat."

And then he thought better of it. It was best to stay out of temptation's way. "I'll take a rain check," he finally told her.

"Up to you. The lasagna'll be there if you change your mind."

After hanging up, she exited the closet-like room humming. Things were definitely looking up.

As she entered the reception area, she saw the back of Shirley's head. Lunch was obviously over.

"First patient is in room one," Shirley announced, handing her the file as she walked by her desk.

Patience nodded. Opening the file as she opened the door, Patience stopped dead in the doorway.

There was a cockatiel in a brightly polished bronze cage on the examination table. A slight, balding man stood beside it, his face a wreath of agony.

Walter Payne.

"Help me," he implored.

Chapter 8

Her mind whirled. What was Walter Payne doing in here?

As if in tune to her thoughts, the cockatiel fluffed up her wings. The bird was obviously ill. Walter must have called in for an appointment. Shirley wasn't aware that Walter had once been guilty of subjecting Patience to unwanted attention. Unwilling to endure the barrage of questions Shirley always asked, she'd put off telling the receptionist to refer Walter to another veterinarian.

Walter's thin features were all but distorted with worry. "Mitzi's sick. She's really sick." He gestured toward the cage helplessly. "Her feathers have been ruffled up like this for over a day and I can't get her to eat anything. I didn't know what to do.'' His eyes pleaded with her. "Please. You helped her before."

Patience hadn't taken a single step into the room. Had Walter made the bird ill on purpose so he would have an excuse to see her again? It could have been as simple a matter as leaving the cockatiel exposed in a draft. Birds caught colds very easily, often with fatal results. If that was the case, then Patience had a great deal to worry about. She knew Walter really loved the bird. If he put Mitzi's life in jeopardy, then he had really gone over the edge.

The folder tucked under her arm, Patience shoved her hands deep into her pockets. Her gaze never wavered from Walter's drawn face. "I can give you the name of a veterinarian who specializes in birds."

He shook his head at her offer. "Whoever it is won't know her like you do," Walter pointed out. "Please. I know you probably don't want me to be here." She'd made that rather clear the last time he'd been here. "And I wouldn't be, but she's sick." His small brown eyes misted behind the rimless glasses. "Mitzi's all I have."

Try as she might to bank it down, Patience could feel sympathy stirring within her. Each and every member of her family would tell her to have the man removed, and from their point of view, they'd be right. But Walter looked so pathetic, pleading with her to save his pet, to ease the bird's suffering. And she *was* a veterinarian. She was bound by her oath, not to mention her honor, to help the bird in any way that she could.

Patience stifled a sigh. "All right, I'll see what I can do." She saw hope enter the man's eyes. "First I need to run some tests." He took a step forward. She stopped him in his tracks. "But I want you to go into the waiting room and stay there until I come out to talk to you." Even if he were harmless, the last thing she wanted was to be alone with him. "Is that understood?"

"Yes, yes." Walter's head bobbed up and down, much the way Mitzi's did when she reacted to the vibrations of a song. "Thank you." His voice cracked. Before leaving the room, he paused by the cage. "The doctor's going to take good care of you, Mitzi. She'll make you well. I promise."

Patience deliberately moved out of the way before he could pass her, then shut the door the second he'd crossed the threshold.

She blew out a slow, shaky breath. This had to stop. She couldn't allow herself to get unsettled like this. What was the matter with her? The man had never even attempted to touch her. But what had touched her were newspaper stories about other women in her situation. Semi-formed scenarios and half-realized fears preyed on her mind. She had to stop doing that to herself.

Taking a deep breath, she turned to face the unhappy cockatiel. "Okay, let's have a look and see what's wrong with you, Mitzi."

When she walked into the reception area forty-five minutes later, several people were waiting with their pets. Walter seemed oblivious to all of them. The second she entered, he popped to his feet like an old-fashioned jack-in-the-box. His small eyes nearly bulged out of his head with anticipation.

"How is she?" Crossing to her, Walter grasped her wrist, then realized what he'd unconsciously done and released her.

"Mitzi has a cold," Patience said. "I gave her some antibiotics." She took a small container of pills out of her pocket, gingerly offering it to Walter. "See that she gets these every six hours, chopped up in her food." She knew how fussy some birds could be. "Mix them in with her fruits and grains, she shouldn't be able to tell the difference. If there's a problem, the medicine also comes in liquid form. Call Shirley if you need them and she'll have some for you at the front desk. You can use an eye dropper to get them down Mitzi's throat. Keep her warm and be sure she stays out of any cross ventilation."

Because there was no other way around it, Patience turned on her heel and led the way to the examination room. Mitzi was in her cage, waiting for her owner.

All the while, as he'd been taking in the information, Walter's head continued to bob up and down. "But she'll be all right?" he asked eagerly as he followed her to collect his pet.

Once on the other side of the examination table, Patience turned to face him. "If you're faithful with her medication, she should be."

Walter made a few cooing noises at the cockatiel, who seemed to listen to them disdainfully. "Do you want to see her for a recheck?"

Ordinarily, Patience would have said yes. She liked to keep tabs on her patients. But in this case, the less she and the bird's owner interacted, the better off she knew her nerves would be. "That shouldn't be necessary."

He beamed at Mitzi, very obviously relieved. "She looks better already. Must be your healing touch."

"It was the antibiotic I gave her," Patience informed him crisply. She nodded at the empty box that had contained the syringe she'd used. "If you forget the instructions, look at the paper that Shirley is going to give you when you go out front again."

Inserting his finger into the cage, something she would have strongly advised against, Walter ran it along the bird's feathers. Ill, the bird still accepted it as her due.

"I don't know how to thank you. I have nothing else in my life besides my work and Mitzi." On her guard, Patience could have sworn she saw longing in the man's eyes. "You know, if things had turned out differently between us—"

"There *was* nothing between us to turn out, Mr. Payne. There was never even an 'us.' Now please, I saw you out of consideration for Mitzi's health, but I'd rather you found another doctor for her."

"There isn't anyone like you."

She was in no mood for flattery, she just wanted him on his way. "Be that as it may, you're going to have to find someone else." She kept her voice as cool and detached as possible. It was against her nature to be hard, but there was no other way. If she left even the smallest of openings, Walter would find a way to wiggle through it.

The man looked as if he wanted to say something else, something in protest, but then he clamped down his mouth. The next moment he picked up the cage, then exited without uttering another word.

Patience was at the door in two strides. She closed it hard, shutting her eyes and trying to pull herself together before the next patient.

After a beat she stepped away from the door. Damn, she wished she were tougher. All those years of putting up a brave front had almost managed to erode her strength. Right now, it felt as if she were walking along a hairy edge, about to plummet over the side.

Nice way for a doctor to behave, she upbraided herself.

The door behind her opened again, and she immediately thought of Walter. Had he fabricated some excuse to return? Not waiting to find out, she grabbed a heavy stone bookend and swung around.

"If you don't go home right now, I'm going to call the police."

Brady stared at her. "I *am* the police. Hey, careful," he cautioned as the bookend slipped from her hands. He reached for it a second too late. "You could lose a toe like that." And then he looked at her ashen face. "What happened?"

Instead of trusting her voice not to break, Patience threw herself into his arms, catching him completely off guard.

She was tired of being brave. She wanted someone else to be brave for her for a change, if only for a second. "Just hold me."

"Okay." He did as she asked. Awkwardly at first and then his arms closed around her more comfortably. The scent of the shampoo she used tripped lightly along his senses, arousing rather than sedating him. He moved the sensation to the rear of his consciousness. "Patience, what just happened here?"

He'd never used her first name before. She'd always been just "Doc." Patience felt tears materializing and silently called herself an idiot. There was no reason to feel this vulnerable. Nothing happened.

This time.

"Walter came."

A tightness formed in Brady's chest. Damn it, he should have talked to the man when she'd told him her story. "What?"

"His bird was sick."

"What?" Hands on her shoulders, Brady held her away from him. Anger joined forces with disbelief as he looked at her.

"Mitzi, his pet cockatiel," she explained. Even as she said it, she felt stupid for being this skittish. And yet she couldn't seem to be able to quite shake off the feeling, couldn't quite get a handle on her resolve. "He wanted me to treat her. He seemed distraught."

"Not as distraught as he's going to be," Brady muttered under his breath.

His words made her rally. She didn't want to start something, she wanted it over with.

Behind her.

Patience squared her shoulders and pulled back. Away from the shelter of his hands, of him. "Brady, I'm all right. I just got upset, that's all."

"Did he try anything?"

"No." She shook her head. "No," she repeated. "He was just grateful I could help Mitzi." And then, because she wanted to be honest about what happened, she added, "He did say that he wished things had turned out better between us."

Storm clouds gathering over the plains appeared

lighter than the expression forming on his face. "I just bet he did."

She pushed her hands deep into her pockets. "Look, I didn't mean to break down like that. I'm just a little punchy, that's all. I haven't been sleeping all that well lately."

There was a lot of that going around, Brady thought, but he said nothing.

"I'm behind," she told him, stepping to the door. Routine. She needed to lose herself in her routine. That was the only way to keep going. And then she paused. He'd told her earlier that he'd take a rain check. What changed his mind? "Why did you stop by?"

"Just to tell you that all the results are in and no one touched the box or card who shouldn't have. The woman at the florist can't remember who ordered the flowers, only that it was paid for in cash." He'd questioned her himself, but had gotten nowhere. According to the man who ran the shop, it had been an unusually busy day.

Patience nodded. "So that's that."

He let her think it was over, but he didn't believe that it was. Most stalkers kept after their target; they didn't just fade graciously away.

"I'll stay on top of it." They walked out into the reception area together. "Be sure and call me if anything turns up."

She flashed him a smile before turning to the next

exam room and her next patient. "Don't take this the wrong way, Coltrane, but I hope I don't have to call you. At least, not about that," she amended.

Brady made no comment, nodding absently as he left.

Walter Payne's address was in his pocket and Brady lost no time in driving over to the man's house. King rode shotgun, alert and taking in this new neighborhood.

"No drug bust here, boy," Brady told the dog. "Just a possible vermin bust."

Walter Payne lived in the oldest part of Aurora. The fifty-plus-year-old neighborhood was comprised of a combination of houses that were either sagging with age and neglect, or beaming with brand-new and relatively brand-new renovations. The Willows, where Payne lived, was a development in transition.

Brady wondered where Payne fit in. He got his answer when he stopped in front of the man's house. Except for a new paint job that, by the looks of it had been done some time in the last few years, the house was sadly in need of major repair. Its entire demeanor appeared dark and forlorn.

Much the way Walter Payne looked when he answered the door after Brady had rung the bell twice. The moment Payne saw the uniform, he straightened, apprehension all but permeating from his every pore. He swallowed audibly before asking, "Yes?"

Brady wasted no time with preliminaries. The man knew why he was here, otherwise he wouldn't look like a frightened rabbit staring at an oncoming eighteen-wheeler. "You come near her again and you're going to be arrested."

There was no need to clarify who he was talking about. They both knew. Payne's broad nostrils flared. It was his only outward sign of bravado. "I only went there because she's Mitzi's doctor."

"Not anymore," Brady informed Payne tersely. As a rule, he was a man of few words. The angrier he became, the fewer the words. "Find another one. Look under V for Vet." His eyes narrowed as he stared down the man. "And vermin."

Payne took a step back into the dark shelter of his home. It seemed as if light refused to cross the threshold or find its way through the windowpanes. "But she—"

"You've had your warning, Payne. Now the choice is yours. And just in case you make the wrong one, remember, a lot of things can happen to someone in the back seat of a squad car before they get to the precinct."

With that, Brady turned away.

Brady heard the door close quickly behind him. The sound of chains being set in place and locks being flipped followed.

A grim smile curved his mouth. He'd done a little background research into Walter Payne. The man was a perfect example of someone who lived a life of quiet frustration. Unless he missed his guess, Payne was the type to pine away after a woman. Violence was a step he wouldn't be willing to take easily. Nothing in his very nondescript life pointed to it. There wasn't so much as a parking ticket with his name on it.

Payne lived modestly and definitely not out of his means. He owned and ran a small, relatively successful computer business. Brady could see how the man could yearn after someone like Patience, but he was reasonably sure that a veiled threat was all that was necessary to get Walter Payne back on track again.

And if not, well, he'd deal with that, too. Nothing got to him faster than a man who threatened a woman's peace of mind.

The rest of his day was uneventful. Brady debated going home after his shift was over. Stretching out in front of the TV with King and a pizza sounded pretty good right about now.

Seeing Patience sounded even better.

He got in behind the wheel of his Mustang and glanced at his watch. According to his estimate, she was calling it a day, as well. There was nothing wrong in stopping by to give her a quick update and a little relief. Despite her words to the contrary and that independent act of hers, he knew she'd been shaken up by Payne's visit and he wanted to assure himself firsthand that she was all right.

"Pizza's on hold, King. We're going by the doc's place first."

King barked his approval.

A grin he reserved only for his furry companion graced Brady's lips. "Sometimes I think you're more human than I am, King."

Again, the dog barked.

Patience was just closing up the clinic when he pulled his car up in the driveway. Seeing him through the window, she stopped and came outside. As he got out of the car, he tried not to let her smile affect him. But it was getting harder and harder to block it.

King was hanging out the window on the passenger side. The canine barked for her attention.

Patience shook her head as Brady approached her. "What did I tell you about letting him hang his head out like that?" She'd given the warning to all five of the officers attached to the K-9 squad.

Brady glanced back at the dog. "It makes him happy. You argue with him."

She crossed her arms in front of her, pretending to scrutinize the officer on her doorstep. "Don't tell me that Officer Coltrane can be manipulated by a furry four-footed animal."

"Let's just say King and I understand each other.
I give him space, he gives me space."

The evening air was crisp, but she hardly felt the
chill. She was warming herself standing beside this
brooding policeman. *I can see right through you,
Brady Coltrane. You're not as tough as you'd like
me to believe.* "Is that what you like, space?"

He shrugged. "I work better that way." At least,
that was what had always worked for him before.
But if that was true, why was he here, in her space,
when he could have been home? After all, he'd
turned down her invitation.

She nodded back toward the building behind her.
"Want to come upstairs for some coffee?"

Yes, he wanted to come upstairs. But not for coffee, which was why he should remain right out here,
where the air was cool and the temptation a little
less intense. Or, if not less intense, at least he
couldn't allow himself to act on it.

He shook his head. "No, I just wanted to make
sure you were all right."

She smiled. "You really are very nice. Sorry—"
Patience raised her hands in mock surrender "—no
compliments, just doing your job, yes, I remember."
She thought of this afternoon. At this point, he prob-
ably thought she was afraid of her own shadow.
"Look, I want to apologize about this whole thing.
I was overreacting—"

He didn't see it that way. What he saw was a

brave woman being justifiably frightened. "No, you weren't. The roses were real, the message was real. That's not overreacting, Doc, that's being sensibly cautious."

Her mouth curved. "If you say so."

He had this overwhelming urge to take her into his arms. To hold her to him and to feel her warmth. But Brady reminded himself he was the one who was supposed to be giving comfort, not the other way around. "I don't think you'll have anything to worry about anymore."

Her eyes narrowed slightly as she looked at him. "What did you do?"

"I went to see Payne."

The wind whipped her hair into her face. She combed it away with he fingers so she could look up at him. "And?"

"And I told him to find another vet. He promised to look."

He'd been coming around with King for two years now. She knew a little something about the way he approached things. "Was this before or after you flipped him and stood on his chest?"

"Before," he quipped, his expression so serious that a look of concern entered her face. How could she be concerned about someone who made her constantly look over her shoulder? What kind of a woman was she? Just how big was her heart?

"Don't worry, I didn't lay a hand on the rodent. But he looked smart enough to be worried."

She laughed, shaking her head. The sound wound itself around him, sealing away the wind. "I would be, too, if you growled at me the way you probably did at him."

This time, when the wind moved her hair into her face, he was the one who combed it away. He watched the pupils of her eyes widen and found himself struggling against falling in. Something tightened in his belly. "You're not the type to be intimidated."

It was what she needed to hear. He made her feel strong, as if everything was going to be all right. And grateful to Brady. "Thanks," she murmured and then, because a part of her still felt vulnerable, still felt the need for someone to turn to, she looked up at him.

Everything she was feeling was in her eyes. He felt himself being drawn in, felt himself wanting to protect her. To keep her out of harm's way for as long as there was breath in his body.

Lightly he slid his hand along her cheek, tilting her head up a little more. He rubbed the tip of his thumb along her lips.

And then, before he knew it, before he could talk himself out of it, he kissed her.

The man watching them from within the shadows swallowed the red-hot curse that burned his throat.

Chapter 9

Patience sighed as she leaned into the kiss, into him. Surprise quickly turned to pleasure. Pleasure turned to desire.

All the fears, all the anxiety that had been dancing around inside of her suddenly burst forth. Overwhelmed by it all, she clung to this tall, dark, silent hero who had stepped out of the shadows into the center stage of her life.

Patience was feeling things, things she'd promised herself she'd never feel for a policeman, never wanted to feel for a man of the law. Or perhaps for any man because feelings like this bound her when she wanted to remain free. But she couldn't dictate to herself now, couldn't reason herself out of what

was happening to her. All she wanted to do was
to feel.

And to lose herself in his arms.

The kiss grew to be all-encompassing and Patience disappeared into it willingly.

Desire came, strong and hard, gripping him by the
chest and spreading swiftly out to the tips of his
limbs. The feeling was alien to Brady, at least to
this degree and with this intensity. Always before,
desire had been physical, to be heeded or not, to be
satisfied or not. The result was never all that overwhelming to him. Passion was something that never
broke through the restraints that he had surrounded
himself with.

But this was different.

This was physical and yet…more. The word intense was not sufficient enough to explain it.

He couldn't explain it. Didn't want to examine it.
Just wanted it to be. Just wanted to keep on kissing
Patience.

He wanted to make love with her.

Damn, he was going to have to watch himself.
Otherwise she'd think he was just using this stalker
thing as an excuse to get her into bed. He couldn't
remember the last time he'd been with a woman.
The whole thing had seemed trivial and uneventful.
Try as he might, he couldn't even remember the
woman's face.

Patience's face was etched in his brain.

He had to stop.

Before he couldn't.

Pulling back, Brady placed his hands on the sides of her shoulders, as if he needed the physical wedge to hold himself in check. When he spoke, his voice was gruff. "You'd better go inside, it's getting chilly."

He watched in complete fascination as the smile in her eyes filtered to her lips. "Not from where I'm standing."

She took a deep breath, trying to clear her head. It was going to take a little more than that, she decided. But Brady was right, she had better go inside before she wound up doing something they'd both regret. She took a step back, seeking the shelter of the doorway. Feeling the chill he was talking about.

"Thanks for stopping by."

It was his suggestion, born of common sense, but he found that he couldn't make himself walk away just yet. "You'll be all right?"

She nodded. "Nothing's going to happen." Digging into her pocket, she produced the card he'd given her the other day, the one with his cell phone number, and held it up. "And if it does, help is only a phone call away."

He'd been thinking of himself instead of her. "Listen, if you're uneasy—"

Patience looked at him for a very long moment. She still felt wobbly.

"Oh, I'm uneasy all right, but Walter Payne has nothing to do with it." And then she grinned. "Worse comes to worst, I can take Walter." She saw Brady raise his eyebrow in a silent question. "Patrick taught me moves guaranteed to make any would-be assailant run for the hills."

"Don't get too confident." He didn't want her letting her guard down. Payne might still surprise them all.

She laughed softly. "Right, that's for someone like you to be."

Brady shook his head. "Too confident is the last thing I am." That kiss had all but destroyed his resolve, showing him just how vulnerable he was. And then, because he had admitted too much, Brady began to leave. "Don't forget to lock up."

"Yes, Officer Coltrane."

He looked at her over his shoulder. She was grinning. Brady shook his head and went to his car. He waited until he heard the chain moved into place and the click of the lock as she flipped it.

The man in the shadows had seen it all, witnessed it all, and cursed the day that the patrolman had ever been born. For one heated moment he thought about taking revenge on him, thought about eliminating the policeman from the mix. Permanently.

But that would just be wasting his time. Because with Coltrane gone, there'd be someone else who'd come along. Someone else she'd want to kiss instead of him.

No, the way to eliminate the competition would be to take Patience away from any temptation. And then she would be his.

Forever.

The way he'd always felt it was meant to be right from the very first time she'd looked at him, standing in the middle of the exam room, so innocent and pure in her white lab coat.

"Soon," he promised himself and the silhouette that appeared in the second-story window. "Soon."

He took out his binoculars.

"Coltrane sent you here, didn't he?"

Josh turned what she could only term as a perfectly confused face toward her when she confronted him with the question a day later. She came to this conclusion when the patrolman and Gonzo had turned up unexpectedly in her exam room.

Josh had apologized for the unscheduled lunchtime visit, but he said he felt that it was justified. He'd noticed Gonzo had been biting his paws a great deal the last couple of days. A close examination of the dog's paws failed to reveal the familiar pink hue of a dog chewing on his pads, causing her to feel that Josh had fabricated the excuse just to look in on her. That meant it was Brady's doing and that she was now under unofficial police protection.

There was no other assumption she could logically make and while this was sweet and comforting in its own way, this "protection" also interfered with her practice. It was one thing to care for the K-9 unit when there was an emergency, but quite another when she did it for no other reason than because she needed looking out for.

Josh frowned. "Why would Coltrane have anything to do with Gonzo's sore paws?"

She crossed the initial notation she'd made in the dog's chart and tossed the file onto the side counter. "Because Gonzo's paws look perfectly fine to me."

"He just started chewing on them. A couple of days ago," Josh added.

He was lying, Patience thought, but she played along with it since what she proposed would do no harm to the animal. She opened a cabinet and took out a small pump bottle, then offered the same to Josh.

"Okay, then spray this on his paws when you get home this evening. That should discourage him."

Josh turned the bottle around in his hand without bothering to read the small print on the side. "What is it?"

"Bitter apple spray." She pet the animal's side. "He gets a mouthful of that, he's not going to want to repeat the experience."

Nodding absently, Josh slipped the small bottle into his pocket. Gonzo's snacking habits, real or otherwise, wasn't the reason he was here. "Listen, if you're not busy later on tonight, maybe you can show me how to spray it on properly."

Humor quirked her mouth. Noble purpose notwithstanding, nothing seemed to discourage Josh from trying to wear her down. "And while I'm at it, maybe I should spray a little bitter apple on myself to discourage you." She picked up Gonzo's file again, intending to deposit it on the front counter for Shirley to file. "You graduated from college, Josh, I think you can figure out how to use a spray."

His eyes washed over her. "C'mon, Patience, why don't you give us a try? You never know, you might like going out with me. People do change their minds about things all the time."

"I won't." She saw his face harden. "It's not you, Josh, it's the principle of the thing. I can't get involved with a policeman, that's all there is to it. I already worry about my uncles, my brother and my cousins. I don't want to have to worry about someone I'm involved with, too. It would be too much for me to handle."

His expression conveyed doubt, as if for the first time since he'd known her, he didn't believe her. "So you're not involved with Coltrane?"

The question caught her off guard. "Involved? No." Had he seen something in her eyes, something she didn't want to even admit to herself? "What makes you say that?"

He shrugged. Rubbing Gonzo's head, he kept his eyes on her. "Just a hunch. I've seen the way he looks at you."

There'd been nothing there for her to detect. Yes, he'd kissed her, or kissed back when she'd kissed him, but that only meant he was human. "What, like I'm an annoyance?"

"That's not what I'd call it." He gave the dog's leash a tug and Gonzo jumped from the table. Josh took the bottle out of his pocket and looked at it. For now, he seemed to give up trying to change her mind. "So, how many times a day do I need to spray his feet?"

She was relieved the conversation had taken a different route. "Just at night, unless you notice him really going at them during the day."

He nodded, pocketing the small bottle again. "He's too busy during the day busting bad guys. So am I," he told her. "See you around, Patience."

But Patience was already out the door, on to her next patient.

After a moment, Josh left the room, as well.

She debated calling Brady.

But each time that she reached for the telephone receiver, she made herself put it down. The game of mental hot potato went on for a day, until she told herself that she was behaving like an idiot. What she meant to suggest was strictly for Brady's own good. She was calling him purely for altruistic reasons, nothing more.

Altruism and because she was feeling very good. There'd been no more flowers on her doorstep, no poems or cards to be wary of. The only conclusion she could make was that her ''admirer'' had been Walter and whatever Brady had said to the man had obviously borne fruit. Although she had learned to be cautious when it came to things within her private life, she was beginning to feel that perhaps that whole ugly episode was finally behind her.

And if it was, it was because of Brady.

She wanted him to know how grateful she was for the way he had discreetly handled everything. Uncle Andrew and Aunt Rose were throwing a party. Shaw, their oldest son, and his wife had just had a baby girl and Uncle Andrew, never reticent when it came to an excuse for throwing a party, was pulling out all the stops. The last time she'd checked, it seemed as if their immediate corner of the world was invited. She knew for a fact that an invitation had been posted on the board on the first floor of the precinct. She also knew, going by her gut feeling, that Brady wouldn't pay any attention to it. And he should. Because she felt that being around a large, loving, albeit boisterous family

might be just what Brady needed after missing out
on this in his childhood.

"What do you say, girl, shall we call him?" she
asked Tacoma. She took the dog tilting her head as
agreement.

Patience picked up the receiver before she could
talk herself out of it again.

Brady answered on the second ring. "Hello?"

Patience felt something flutter in her throat. Probably her heart. It had obviously decided to relocate.
Altruistic my foot, she thought.

"Hi, it's Patience."

"What's wrong?"

She heard the tension in his voice. A twinge of
guilt waltzed through her. She should have prefaced
her greeting with a disclaimer that nothing was happening to force her to make the call. That she
wanted to make this call.

"Nothing, I just wanted to call and invite you."

There was a significant pause on the other end,
and she thought for a second that he'd lost the signal. And then she heard him ask, "To what?"

Patience took a deep breath. She made it a point
to always be friendly and outgoing. This should
have been as easy as falling off a log for her. So
why did she feel as if her palm was growing damp
against the telephone receiver?

"Uncle Andrew's having a party to celebrate my
cousin Shaw's new baby. Patrick said there was an

invitation posted on the ground-floor board. I thought maybe, you being you, you might have missed it.''

As a matter of fact, he hadn't. He'd just chosen to ignore it because large social gatherings weren't his thing. After hours he kept to himself, preferring King's company to anyone else's.

Or at least he had.

"No," he told her quietly, "I didn't miss it."

She waited. Nothing. She thought about the old line about leading a horse to water. In this case, it was dragging, not leading, and the horse had all the markings of a mule.

"So," she finally said, "are you going?"

"No."

She frowned to herself. "Why not?"

"I didn't realize it was mandatory."

She sighed. Why did this have to be so difficult? "It's not, but don't you ever loosen up?"

"I run on the beach with King."

"That's not loosening up, Coltrane, that's exercise. You can bring King, you know. He is part of the police department and my uncle loves dogs." She had a feeling Josh would be there, as he had on other occasions when her uncle had had an open house. Most likely, he would bring Gonzo with him. The dog was good with children. "Why don't you ask King? Maybe he'd like to come."

"King and I like being on our own."

She'd hoped to coax a smile out of him, but if there was one, she didn't hear it in his voice. Patience paused, knowing she was going out on a limb. She crawled out on it anyway.

"I'd like you to come. Both of you." He said nothing. "Or just send King if you're busy."

"We'll see."

She knew what that meant. It had been one of Patrick's favorite phrases. "That's a polite way of saying no, isn't it?"

"Maybe."

She could just picture him on the other end, scowling into the telephone. "Well, I can't make you, but I really think it would do you good."

"And why is that?"

"Because I think you need to see that not every family is dysfunctional. That sometimes parents really do love each other and their kids. That that's the norm and not something else." Again there was silence on the other end of the line. For so long that she finally ventured, "Brady? Are you there?"

"Yeah, I'm here." His voice was tight with emotions that were not allowed to break free. "What makes you think I need to see that?"

"Because I needed to see it, to feel it," she told him.

Didn't he realize that she understood him better than he thought? Understood him because she'd lived through what he had. She'd already told him about her childhood, about the father who had colored her world in dark shades, just as his had. Why couldn't Brady see that she just wanted him to get past that? To find his own place among people, not somewhere out in the desert like a brooding hermit.

"Being around Uncle Andrew and his family was what helped keep me going when I was a little girl."

"I'm not a little girl."

She nearly laughed at that, but knew he hadn't said it to be funny. "No, you're definitely not that." She paused, searching for the right words. "But we all carry around the child we were inside. And children need to be reassured from time to time."

When he spoke again, there was finally a hint of tolerant humor in his voice. "Being a shrink again?"

"Being a friend," she corrected. "I thought we established that, that we're friends." She sighed, knowing that any further argument would just fall on deaf ears. "It's tomorrow at one. I'll be leaving at twelve-thirty if you change your mind."

"I won't."

"No," she murmured, "I don't expect you will."

Well, she thought as she hung up, she'd tried. Somehow the thought wasn't very comforting. She hated failing.

Dawdling. There was no other term for it. She was dawdling. She'd been ready for more than half an hour, even moving at the slow pace she'd adopted. She'd even wrapped the gift she was bringing for the baby in what amounted to slow motion.

No one rang her bell. No one called.

He wasn't coming.

Big surprise.

Tacoma nosed at her as she glanced out the window for the umpteenth time. When she looked at the pet, the animal gave her that funny, quizzical look she was wont to offer whenever she felt that her mistress was acting against type.

"Can't fool you, can I?" she laughed.

Usually she'd be out the door way ahead of time, especially when a family gathering was involved. She liked helping out, liked setting up. It wasn't just the food that was the allure. No doubt the food was always spectacular, but it was the company that drew her. There wasn't a single person in her extended family that she didn't get along with. And she loved catching up on what everyone was doing.

When she was younger, she'd turned to them for mute comfort, something just being around them accomplished. She genuinely loved each and every one of them and took great pleasure out of being involved in their lives. They were all good people.

She knew that her uncles could have easily ignored what was happening in her house, but they hadn't. Especially not Andrew. Andrew had taken it upon himself to try to straighten out his younger brother. Time and again he'd come over late at night after her mother had tearfully summoned him following one of her father's drinking binges. Uncle Andrew would stay up with her father, talking until the wee hours of the morning, trying to get at the root of his insecurities. It had been to no avail. But until the day her father had been killed in the line of duty, her uncle never gave up trying. Despite everything, her father had remained a loner, alone in a large family.

Was that how it was with Brady? she wondered. Was he destined to go through life alone? Not her problem. No one could change anyone, that had to come from within. She just had to accept that.

She glanced at her watch. If she wasn't careful, she was going to be late. Picking up the present, she headed for the door.

"C'mon, girl, let's go."

Swinging open the door, juggling leash and gift, she walked right into him. Patience bit back a scream. But it wasn't Walter.

Brady was on her doorstep.

Chapter 10

It took her less than half a second to recover. Beside her, Tacoma was jumping from side to side, joyously greeting master and pet. Patience held on to the leash as best she could. "You changed your mind."

Because it looked as if Tacoma was going to pull her down in her enthusiasm, Brady took the leash from Patience. "Something like that."

A sense of pleasure filled her and she smiled at him. "Good."

"Yeah, well, we'll see." Brady glanced at the gift she was holding, a large box with a white-pink ribbon. "I don't have anything to give them."

"No problem, we'll put your name on this, too."

Before he could protest, Patience pulled a pen out of her purse and added his name to the card tucked under the ribbon.

The woman worked fast, he thought with a shake of his head. She made retreat impossible. Brady nodded at the gift as she dropped the pen back into her purse. "What do I owe you?"

Patience waved away the offer. "We'll settle up later." And then she glanced toward the driveway where his car was parked beside hers. She could picture him having a change of heart five feet from Uncle Andrew's house. "Why don't we take my car since I know the way? Besides, there's going to be a sea of cars in the area. Parking one extra vehicle's going to be challenge, much less two. And I wouldn't want to see anything happen to your pretty car."

"I could turn around and go home."

She could have slipped her arm through his, but she relied on her own power of persuasion instead. Patience pinned him with a look as she asked sweetly, "And just what makes you think I'll let you go after you've come this far?"

Brady pulled himself up to his full height. There was less than a foot between them only because she wore four-inch heels. But she still looked small.

"Don't see that there's anything you can do about it if I change my mind." Rather than answer, she watched him steadily. Brady relented. "Okay, your car."

And then she grinned that grin of hers, the one that went straight to his bones and filtered out into all his extremities, making him feel just the slightest bit weak. Just the slightest bit invaded, but in a good way. Brady knew he was going to regret this.

But he had to go.

Andrew Cavanaugh, the former chief of the Aurora Police Department and present host of what both he and those around him felt were the largest, best parties in the city, greeted them at the door when they arrived twenty minutes later. Checking on some of his guests, Andrew had passed by the bay window that looked out onto the front lawn when he saw his niece, a man he vaguely recognized, and two dogs coming up the front walk. It was enough to catch his attention.

Patience did not bring men to the house. Ever.

Before his niece could ring the bell, the door swung open and Andrew embraced her as if he hadn't just seen her at the breakfast table less than three days ago. He nearly crushed the present she carried.

"Patience, come on in," he told her with enthusiasm the second he released her from the bear hug. "Patrick, Maggi and the little one are already here."

"Well, that's a switch," she laughed. "Patrick

was always the holdout.'' Marriage and fatherhood had drastically changed her brother, all for the good. She slanted a side glance toward Brady. ''A little like you were trying to be.''

Holding on to both her dog and his partner, Brady made no comment.

Andrew sized him up quickly. Twenty-eight years on the job had taught him well and honed his abilities to a fine point. ''And you're...Brady Coltrane.''

Mild surprise flickered through Brady's eyes as he glanced at her. Patience knew he was asking her how her uncle knew he'd be here when even *he* hadn't known that until he'd turned up on her doorstep.

''Someone must have pointed you out to Uncle Andrew at one time or another. Uncle Andrew's got a photographic memory,'' Patience explained.

''Actually,'' Andrew conceded, ''I recognized the dog.'' He nodded at King. ''Fine animal.'' He allowed King to smell his hand before he ran it over the dog's head. ''Josh is already here.'' He nodded in the general direction he'd seen the other man in the last time he'd looked. ''He brought Gonzo so the three of them should have a good time.'' He pretended to take Patience to one side and suggested in a stage whisper, ''Why don't you see if you can do the same for Officer Coltrane?''

Brady looked around, missing the light pink hue

that filtered along her cheeks. He was too busy having misgivings about what unchecked impulse had caused him to come here.

He looked like a man one step away from bolting. She could read him, Patience thought as she shifted and leaned into Brady. "I admit this takes a bit of getting used to. Maybe I should have started you out small, like inviting you to breakfast."

"Breakfast?" Brady looked at her quizzically.

"Uncle Andrew likes to have the family over for breakfast every morning." There was a giant, custom-made table in the kitchen that they were quickly outgrowing now that marriage and procreation had entered the Cavanaugh picture. "Anywhere from two to twenty-two people show up on any given day."

"Twenty-three," Rose Cavanaugh, a serene-looking blonde with lively eyes, interjected as she joined them and slipped her arm through Andrew's, "if you count Shaw's baby."

"Of course we'll count Shaw's baby. Why shouldn't we count the newest member of the family?" Andrew asked.

Her face glowed as she looked up at Andrew. Rose Cavanaugh was clearly a woman in love with her husband. "He takes his family very seriously," she confided to Brady.

Brady felt himself responding to the woman's warm smile. Though they were related only by marriage, he felt that Patience had a lot in common with her aunt. He knew he should leave now, while the getting was still good. "So I've heard."

"Make yourself at home," Andrew instructed. Callie waved to him from across the room, beckoning her parents over. Andrew began moving in that general direction. "Let me know if there's anything you want," he told Brady as he melded into the crowd with his wife.

"Other than to leave," Patience whispered against Brady's ear.

Brady looked at her as if she'd just read his mind and she couldn't help laughing at his expression. "How did you know?"

She stopped to pick up two canapés from a tray. Everywhere she looked, there were people and food. It was a hungry crowd. She fed the meat-filled canapés to the dogs before looking at Brady.

"You forget, I have the advantage of having Patrick as a brother. He resisted becoming part of all this for a long time. But he finally surrendered. Being part of this family soothed most of the wounds he'd been carrying around." She spotted her brother and his wife over in a corner. Patrick had the baby on his lap. "Maggi took care of the rest."

"Maggi?"

"His wife. Detective Mary Margaret McKenna," she elaborated. Some people referred to her sister-in-law as "3M." Patience referred to her as a saint because Maggi made her brother so happy.

Brady knew the name. Maggi McKenna had been a native to Aurora, leaving for a while to work with the San Francisco police before transferring back to Aurora when her father, a patrolman, was shot on the job. No one knew she was with Internal Affairs until she'd been assigned to investigate rumors that Patrick Cavanaugh was a dirty cop. She'd wound up clearing his reputation, marrying him and transferring to vice. He'd heard that all of the former police chief's kids had a similar story to tell, their jobs leading them to love in one way or another.

Made for good stories to swap, but things like that didn't happen to people like him. His was a different world.

What are you thinking, Brady? Why is tension never far away from you?

Patience fixed her best smile into place. "Why don't you take that frown off your face and relax a while, Coltrane?" she suggested. "I promise you dinner will be worth the trip here."

If he was about to comment, his words were swallowed up as Josh came up behind them and placed a hand on each of their shoulders. Gonzo barked as all three dogs clustered around them, sniffing at each other. Patience made a mental note to get all three dogs out into the yard where they could run free.

"I thought I saw you two coming in." Josh

looked from one to the other, his expression that of mild surprise. "You two come together?"

Patience read between the lines and kept her answer light. "He didn't know the way. I thought that if I had him follow me, he might make a U-turn and go home."

Brady snorted. "Not a bad guess."

Before Josh could comment, she enlisted his help. "Help me get him to mingle."

Josh paused to give the other man a long, skeptical look. "You know the old saying about leading a mule to water."

"That's horse," Brady corrected.

Josh smirked knowingly. "In your case, Coltrane, it's mule."

She moved in between the two men. "Have you seen Shaw yet?"

Josh's expression softened slightly. "Yeah, over there." He pointed the oldest of Andrew Cavanaugh's offspring out and grinned. "Acting as if he's the first guy who ever fathered a kid."

Brady glanced over toward the far right, saw not only the detective he recognized as one of the Cavanaughs, but also a woman who seemed vaguely familiar to him. For a moment he couldn't place her. And then, the brain being a storage house of all sorts of unused facts, an image from a movie promo clicked into place.

His eyes narrowed as he looked first at the woman, then at Patience. "Isn't that...?"

Patience laughed. This was one of life's little ironies. Shaw met his wife when the latter, doing research for a movie role, had requested a ride-along. He'd agreed to it under duress. Funny how life turned out.

"Moira McCormick. Yes, it is. My somewhat attention-shy cousin wound up marrying a Hollywood movie star." She saw Brady looking around. It didn't take a mind reader to know what he was thinking. "Don't worry, the press is strictly barred from showing up and crashing the party. Uncle Brian would find a reason to have their butts busted and tossed into jail overnight so fast their cameras wouldn't be quick enough to record it."

She rubbed her hand along his arm and found her mouth growing a little dry. She had to force the words out. "Relax, you're among friends."

"Haven't you heard? Coltrane doesn't have any friends beside his dog," Josh quipped.

"We're here to fix that," Patience cheerfully informed the other patrolman. But she wasn't about to accomplish this with Josh shadowing her every move. She had the distinct feeling that she was the unwilling participant in a tug-of-war. And Josh was tugging a lot harder than Brady was.

She needed help.

Scanning the room, she found and made eye contact with her cousin, Janelle. Uncle Brian's only daughter was an assistant in the D.A.'s office. Growing up, she and Janelle had been on a special wavelength. Patience could only hope that some things didn't change just because they were older now.

It took a moment, but then she watched her cousin disengage herself from the person she was talking to and make her way toward them. Patience secretly blessed Janelle.

The relief in Patience's eyes might not have been evident to some people, but Janelle felt as if she knew her cousin inside and out. Besides, the dilemma was easy to spot. Patience had one too many men at her side. Judging by her stance, Janelle knew which one was the spare and which was not. If she was surprised about Patience's choice of dates—policemen—she gave no indication.

The moment she reached them, Janelle turned her attention to the friendlier of the two. "Hi, I'm Janelle Cavanaugh, Patience's cousin, and you're...?"

"Josh Graham."

Janelle reached around Josh to get a glass of wine. The maneuver was shameless and she knew it, but she was doing it to bail Patience out and that was enough to assuage her conscience.

"So—" she lifted the glass to her lips "—what do they have you doing in the police department, Josh?"

"He's with the K-9 unit," Patience told her. "The bomb squad."

"Really?" Janelle's peaches-and-cream complexion grew a little rosier as she registered rapt attention. "Why don't we take these three outside where they can run around a bit?" She hooked her arm through Josh's. "Tell me, how do you get a dog to find a bomb?" With a minimum of effort, she had man and dogs halfway across the room, heading for the patio.

I owe you, Janey, she thought, taking her hat off to Janelle. She turned to Brady, who looked a little bemused by the quick extraction. "My cousin works at the D.A.'s office."

He laughed dryly. "I'd hate to show up on the wrong side of her table." The woman was clearly a master at anything she undertook. Picking up two glasses of wine, he handed one to Patience. "So, what was all that really about?"

She thought of denying any knowledge of what he was talking about, but that was just absurd. Besides, she liked the fact that he wasn't easily dazzled. "So you caught that. I got the feeling you and Josh weren't exactly buddies. So I called for help."

"How, through mental telepathy?"

"Janelle and I can usually guess what the other's thinking. Comes in handy."

"I'll bet." Brady shrugged, thinking of her comment about Josh. "Graham's all right." He said the words without feeling. He and the other policeman had had about five or so conversations in total, with Graham doing most of the talking. "He seems to be interested in you."

"Josh is always asking me out." She shrugged. "I figure it's all in good fun."

He studied her for a moment as he took a sip of wine. "Then you've gone out with him?"

"No." Her eyes met his. "I don't go out with policemen."

"I see. Then this is—"

"A party," she answered simply, then felt she needed to add the real reason behind her invitation. "And a way to show you that families can get along."

"What makes you think I need to see that?" He saw the knowing look that came into her eyes. He didn't want anyone trying to make him reassess his life. He'd already come to terms with it, both past and present. Which meant he knew what his future would be like. More of the same. He turned from her as he took another long sip. "Why don't you just stick to treating animals?"

She grinned. "I kinda thought I was." Eyeing her, Brady opened his mouth to retort, then found himself laughing. "Good," Patience pronounced. "You have a nice laugh. Now, let's go say hi to Shaw and Moira so I can unload this present. And then I'll get you started on one of Uncle Andrew's hors d'oeuvres.''

Taking the box from her to enable her mobility, Brady let her take the lead. She wove her way toward the guests of honor like a freshly released arrow, all the while holding on to his hand. She'd taken it without a word. His first instinct was to pull back, but he kept his hand where it was, with her fingers around his. He savored the contact and told himself he was an idiot.

The crowd around Shaw and Moira turned out to be too thick to penetrate.

Patience looked at Brady over her shoulder. ''We'd need a bulldozer to get through. Maybe later.'' She saw a huge pile of gifts not far off. She handed him the one she'd brought. ''Just put that over there,'' she instructed.

''Any other orders?'' he asked after he dropped off the gift.

She grinned again, wounding him without drawing a drop of blood, and slipped her hand over his one more time. ''Yeah, follow me.''

This time, she led him into the kitchen. For once it was empty. Almost. She stopped short as she came up on her uncle nuzzling his wife.

Her eyes danced as she looked back at Brady. Everyone in the family thought of what had happened to Andrew and Rose as their own personal miracle. ''Looks like food isn't the only thing cooking in here." Patience put her hand up in front of her face to pretend to block her view of the couple. "Sorry about that."

"Don't be," Andrew laughed. Still holding the woman he loved close, he threaded his arm around her waist. "I'm not." He looked up at Patience and the man who had clearly caught his niece's fancy, whether she was willing to admit it or not. "What can I get you two?"

"One of your canapés to start with. I promised Brady an experience he'd remember a long time," Patience said.

Andrew gave his niece a long, significant look and then smiled.

"All right. I've got a fresh tray right there. Do me a favor and take it out to the crowd, will you?" he asked Patience. And then his eyes shifted toward his wife. "I've got a little pressing, unfinished business to tend to first."

"Will do." Reaching for the tray, she smiled when Brady picked it up for her and started for the living room. She quickly followed in his wake. "Thanks."

"How long have they been married?" he asked her once they were clear of the kitchen.

"Over thirty years," she told him. "But he's just recently found her again and I guess they're like newlyweds right now." She glanced back toward the kitchen and didn't bother hiding the sigh that escaped. If only her own parents had been half as much in love, maybe things would have turned out differently for all of them. She pushed the thought from her mind as she glanced back at Brady. "I think it's sweet."

He'd forgotten about that. The resolution to the fifteen-year-old case had been in all the local papers. Rose Cavanaugh had driven off one morning fifteen years ago after an argument with her husband, only to disappear. Her car was found in the river the next day and it was assumed by everyone but the chief that her body had been washed out to sea. He never once gave up hope that he'd find her someday. Years later, he did. She had been working as a waitress in a diner up the coast. A blow to the head and her harrowing near-death experience in the river had caused her to lose her memory, something obviously in the past now, he thought.

How did it feel to have someone come back from the dead? he wondered. An emotion vaguely resembling envy fluttered through him before disappearing. He couldn't have these normal feelings, normal reactions. He had to remember that.

"I guess your uncle was lucky."

She noted the wistful tone in his voice and wondered at it. At least this made him human, she thought. "Guess so."

He had to admit it. Dinner was everything Patience had promised. And more. The former chief of police knew his way around a kitchen. Brady couldn't remember when he'd eaten a better meal. Everything he had was even better than the last. He had no idea why the Cavanaughs didn't all weigh in at three hundred pounds.

More impressive than the meal was the company. Granted most of the department, active and retired, had been invited, but he'd never seen people get along the way Patience's relatives did. Love seemed to echo from every corner, every pore. Not the sickeningly sweet kind but the living, breathing, you're-my-brother-sister-cousin-child and I'd-go-to-hell-and-back-twice-for-you kind.

Something he'd never felt. Or, if he had, it was only in a small way. On a lonely road.

But he also had to get going. He could only be in the presence of a happy, functional environment for so long before he needed space.

He and Patience were sitting outside, on the patio. She saw him shift restlessly. He'd lasted longer than she'd thought he would. "Time to go?" she guessed, watching his face.

"You don't have to leave on my account," he told her. "I'll get a ride with someone."

Abandoning her seat, she managed to match him stride for stride. "That's all right. Let's just go get the dogs. I'm tired."

He knew she was lying, but said nothing.

* * *

The ride back was conducted in basic silence. She tried to coax him into a conversation once, then decided to let him have a few minutes of quiet. God knew he'd earned it. When they reached her driveway, she half expected master and dog to bound out of the car together, head for their own vehicle and leave.

That he walked her to her door was a bonus she hadn't expected. Tacoma led the way, with King bringing up the rear. She was aware only of Brady.

Digging out her key, she turned toward him. "I'm glad you came," she told him. "Very glad."

"Yeah," Brady half mumbled under his breath. "Me, too."

She didn't believe him, but she wanted to. "Really? They can be kind of overwhelming when taken en masse like that, but no matter what happened at home, they always made me feel like I belonged. Made me feel loved."

He paused, wanting to kiss her, knowing he shouldn't. For both their sakes. She didn't want to get involved with a policeman and he just didn't want to get involved, period. But he could feel himself weakening.

What came out, did so out of the blue. Purely a defense mechanism meant to cut himself off from her. "I shot my father," he said without any preamble.

She stared at him, stunned, trying to figure out how she should react to this. "Excuse me?"

"My father," Brady repeated. "I shot him." He looked at her for a long moment. "I just thought you might want to know that before you go any further with whatever you think you're doing for my own good."

She tried to reconcile the man standing in front of her with the information he'd just given her. She couldn't.

"You shot him?"

"Yes."

"Intentionally?"

He smiled then. It wasn't the kind of question that first came to mind for a lay person. "Easy to see you've got police in your background."

"Answer the question. Did you kill him on purpose?"

For a second he allowed himself to go back to a time that was worse than living in hell.

"I must have killed him a thousand times in my mind. Just as many times as I rescued my mother from him and talked her into running away with us. With Laura and me." He'd done neither. He blew out a breath, looking into the night. When he turned his eyes back in her direction, he seemed calmer and in control. "But did I aim the gun at him that night, dead center and pull the trigger? No. That was an accident."

Her mouth was bone-dry. ''What kind of an accident?'' she asked. ''Handling-the-gun-and-it-went-off kind of accident?''.

''No, more like wrestling-the-old-man-and-trying-to-get-the-gun-out-of-his-hand-before-he-killed-someone-worth-mourning kind of accident.'' He sighed. Try as he might, there were no regrets. His father had been a man who hadn't deserved to live. ''It went off. Hitting him in the chest. He was dead before he ever reached the hospital.''

Things fell into place. She wanted to hold him, to embrace him and to tell him it was all right. ''Do you want to come inside?''

''It's late.''

''I didn't ask you for the time.''

''No, I guess you didn't.''

She took a step back, the invitation reinforced. ''So?''

Brady followed her inside without another word.

Chapter 11

The moment the door closed behind them, they knew. Knew this wasn't a time for conversation, for words that were meant to soothe but came a distant second to true desire. They needed the comfort that came through touch, through the most basic of physical contact.

Through the mingling of bodies and, just perhaps, of souls.

Behind him, Brady heard the click of the lock as the door met the jamb. Hurting from memories he'd long since thought buried, he swept Patience into his arms and kissed her. Kissed her the way he'd been longing to for what felt like an eternity.

The neediness within Brady had brought him to

a point of vulnerability he'd never experienced before, even at the lowest point of his childhood. Tomorrow there would be self-reprisals and regrets, but
right now he needed this, needed to lose himself in
this feeling, in this woman. He knew in his heart
that none of this was real and that there was no
salvation at the end of the path, but for now, he
could pretend to believe in that. Believe in the sheer
purity this woman represented.

Believe in salvation.

Her world was so different from his, had been so
different from his. Because, no matter what, there
had been love for her to grow on. The way there
hadn't been for him.

He couldn't remember ever feeling love. Couldn't
remember ever feeling anything but a sense of duty
toward his mother and sister, because they'd had no
one else. For his father, he'd felt nothing but hatred,
such enormous hatred.

He gave as good as he'd gotten.

He wanted to be cleansed. To forget, just for a
moment, that he was this man who couldn't feel.
Who had no love to offer, no evidence of love in
his life. He wanted to cross the border and to quietly
slip out of his world into hers.

The heat of the kiss grew, spreading all through
him, absorbing him into the fire. Cleansing him.

With a hesitation that was completely foreign to
him, Brady touched her, letting his fingers trail along

her back, up her sides. Anticipating the press of flesh against flesh. The swell of her breasts, pressed so urgently against him, filled him with both desire and a sense of sweetness that came from nowhere and left him in awe and wonder.

Things happened inside of him, things he couldn't understand. Things beyond the physical.

Sounds filled his head. Distant noises that steadily became louder.

Whining?

Moaning?

And then he felt Patience press her palms against his arms, pushing him back. Not urgently, but just enough to make him stop.

Reality dawned on him. What the hell was he doing? An apology hovered on his lips, but the look in her eyes was amusement. He didn't understand.

"We have an audience," she told him. When he said nothing, just watched her, Patience nodded her head toward the two dogs who sat side by side like a furry Greek chorus not two feet away, watching their every move. Tacoma made a high-pitched noise that sounded very much like whining. Something akin to a rumbling noise came from King. "I think Tacoma's jealous."

"Of me?" Brady felt as if his brain was encased in a fog.

He watched as a smile rose into her eyes. Desire crescendoed inside his belly. He wanted nothing more than to stand here and bask in the light, in the warmth he felt emanating from her.

"No," Patience corrected. "Of me. I think she likes you. A lot. She wants to be the alpha female." And then she blew out a breath as if she were trying to get her bearings. He could identify with that, he thought. Cupping her hand to his cheek, she said, "Whatever you're thinking, hold that thought. I'll be right back." She looked at the two dogs. "C'mon, you two. Your masters need some alone time."

Aching for her, Brady watched as she led the two dogs away to another room. He heard a door close somewhere down the hall. She was back in less than a minute.

For the sake of future tranquillity, he tried to talk himself out of making love with her. And had very little success.

"Okay," Patience said cheerfully as she presented herself in front of him again, "where were we?"

He wanted to frame an apology, something about being carried away by the moment and the import of what he'd just shared with her on her doorstep. The words refused to come and then they were halted altogether. The very air stopped in his lungs as she took his hand and placed it on her breast.

"I believe you were here," she told him, rising

just slightly on her toes. "And your mouth—" she moved closer "—was right here."

Like a man in a dream, he felt his heart all but stop. Felt her breath on his lips. Felt everything within him tightening like a wet leather string left out in the sun. He'd never wanted someone so much in his life, couldn't remember *ever* wanting anyone the way he wanted her.

And it scared him. Scared him because it took control out of his hands and placed it in hers. "Patience—" he began.

"Yes," she whispered, "we've both exercised more than a little of it. Now it's time to act on the way we both feel."

He wanted nothing more than to take her. But he'd always been aware of consequences and in this case there were huge ones. For both of them, her as well as him. "You're going to regret this."

"Only if I stop." Feeling so much she didn't know where to begin, Patience tried very hard to contain it all and to move forward slowly. But move forward she would. Because to step back at this point was unthinkable. Her eyes held his. "Rule Number One. Don't ever, ever, tell me how I'm going to react to something—because you have no way of knowing."

He feathered his fingers through her hair. Golden highlights gleamed at him from the strawberry strands. "I thought Rule Number One was no policeman."

A very sexy grin curved the corners of her mouth. "You're not wearing a uniform right now," she pointed out. Then, surprising herself a little and him a great deal, she began to unbutton his shirt. Slowly. Seductively. She could feel his pulse drumming beneath her fingers. "And pretty soon, you won't be wearing anything at all."

Whatever control he thought he had over himself shattered into a thousand pieces. Needs began to urgently pound through him, demanding satisfaction. Demanding her.

Hardly knowing what he was doing, he found the zipper at the back of her dress and pulled it down to its base. The turquoise fabric seemed to sigh right off her body. Sigh the way he realized he had as he saw her standing in a lacy white bra, matching panties and stockings that seemed to have no earthly way of staying up.

Excitement tightened like a fist within his belly. He felt himself hardening even more.

It took him a second to reassure himself that he hadn't swallowed his own tongue.

The rest was a haze of feelings, of desires and near fulfillments. He took off her bra and panties, teasing them both, but left her stockings in place. She was incredibly erotic, wearing only the soft scraps of nylon. His own clothes were shed in a flurry as the need to feel her flesh against his grew more urgent.

He explored her, even as she explored him, and they both drove one another almost crazy as they touched, caressed and pressed moist, openmouthed kisses along trembling skin. He went closer and closer to the edge, only to retreat at the very last moment.

Each time he'd pull himself back from the brink, he did so because he wanted to savor this feeling a little longer. Wanting to pleasure her a little more. It was the only way he could thank her for the respite she was giving him, for dragging him out of the solitary world that he had inhabited for so long.

Patience twisted and turned beneath his touch, beneath the hot trail that his mouth was forging. Biting back moans.

Damn, but she had never thought it could be like this. Like fire and ice and shooting stars racing along the sky. Pleasure erupted in her veins over and over again, seemingly joined together in an endless loop that continued to corkscrew all through her. She wanted him with such an intensity she was afraid she was going to explode.

Each time Brady touched her, each time he kissed her, her head spun a little more, her blood heated a little higher.

She wanted to absorb him, to make love with him

like this forever. It had never, ever, occurred to her that it could be this wonderful. Her solitary college experience had been so fraught with such disappointment, she'd come away from it feeling that sex, that lovemaking itself, was highly overrated.

And maybe it was. If it happened with anyone but the right person.

The thought burst across her brain.

Oh no, no, Brady Coltrane wasn't the right person. He couldn't be. She'd promised herself that it would never be a man who lived by the badge.

This had to be sorted out.

Later.

For now, Brady remained the most dynamic man she had ever met. And so very skilled at what he did. Because he played her as if she were a fine, rare instrument, making her body hum. Making every single inch of her vibrate. With longing. With anticipation.

She wrapped her legs around him, moving the core of her against him. She didn't know how much longer she could last like this.

They were on the floor and then, suddenly, he was over her. She could feel him wanting her. Her heart was pounding so hard, she could scarcely breath.

Now, her eyes implored him. *Make love with me now!*

And then, just as she was certain she was going to expire, she felt him enter her. Felt the sweet, overpowering sensation as he sheathed himself within her. She raised her hips up urgently, meeting him halfway. Beginning the movement that would ultimately bring them down from the summit they were climbing.

His eyes were on hers, as if he were trying to memorize her every feature, her every breath. Mesmerized, she didn't even blink.

Brady moved harder and harder, needing release and yet, at the same time, not wanting this time to end. He wanted her with such force that it all but completely undid him.

When the climax came, seizing both of them in its grip, he tightened his arms around her, as if he meant to pull her into him, to make her a permanent part of himself.

He tried to absorb her into his very skin, feeling things that he couldn't put into words even if he'd wanted to try.

As the sensation slowly began to ebb away, he continued to hold her to him, vainly trying to prolong the moment.

But eventually it flowed on the wings of night.

She had trouble regulating her breathing. Everything still raced inside her, breaking every speed record. Finally she turned toward him and saw an odd look on his face.

So many things were going on inside, he couldn't

begin to catalog them, couldn't begin to even pick his way through them. "Doc—"

So, it was Doc again, not Patience, she thought. She tried to brace herself and knew she wasn't going to do a very good job of it.

There was a smile on her lips, but this time it didn't reach her eyes.

"Coltrane," she warned him, "if you apologize for this, I swear I'm going to make a necklace out of your teeth."

The absurd image made him smile, even when there was nothing to smile about. Because he'd weakened and allowed himself to react to her physically instead of backing away the way he should have.

Unable to help himself, he brushed back a strand of her hair. It was damp with perspiration, like the rest of her. He felt desire stir within him again and he clamped down on it.

"This wasn't supposed to happen." He looked away because looking at Patience only made him want her. Badly.

No, she thought, it wasn't. He was a cop and she wasn't supposed to care about a cop, not in that way. But things didn't always go according to plan. If they had, her father would have been a great deal more loving. And he would have still been alive. So would her mother.

"But it did," she pointed out quietly. She touched

his face, forcing him to look at her. "Don't spoil it by overthinking it, Coltrane. Some things you just have to enjoy. And leave it at that."

As if he could just leave it at that, he silently mocked himself. Before he could say anything to refute what she'd just said, Patience raised her head up and lightly brushed her lips against his. And succeeded in brushing away any noble resolve on his part, as well.

Brady gathered her against him and kissed her. Hard. And the dance began all over again, despite all their resolutions and rules to the contrary.

Patience sighed as she stared at the computer screen. She'd typed the same sentence three times in a row now. It was as if the software was hiccuping. Shaking her head, she pressed the backspace key and deleted the repetitious lines. Finished, she sat back and scrubbed her hands over her face, wishing she could somehow scrub them over her brain, as well.

The past couple of days she'd felt as if she'd been sleepwalking. Sleepwalking and holding her breath. Waiting not for any evidence of the stalker, but some kind of sign that Brady was still in her life.

He'd left that evening soon after they'd made love again. Left quickly with hardly any conversation in his wake. Rather than like lovers, they'd parted like two strangers who'd woken up in the wrong bed. Next to the wrong person.

Was she the wrong person to him?

Was he?

If she looked at the situation logically, she'd made a huge mistake. Except that tiny little voice inside of her kept arguing that she hadn't. But that tiny voice was definitely in the minority. Especially since Brady hadn't called since he'd walked out her door.

Face it, she told herself. It was just one of those things that happen. It's over, finished before it really started.

But, whether she liked it or not, her one night of lovemaking was going to become a yardstick by which she would measure every other man. Because, whatever else he might be, Brady Coltrane was a fantastic lover. Kind, gentle and stirring beyond belief. And no matter what else happened in her life, she was always going to remember the night they'd had together.

Disgusted with the fact that she couldn't seem to focus her thoughts for more than thirty seconds at a time, she began to power down her computer.

As her fingers hit the appropriate keys, a question flashed across the screen.

"No, I don't want to save Document 1," Patience told the screen. "It's all hodgepodge anyway." Served her right for trying to update files when her mind had taken a powder.

"Um, Dr. Cavanaugh?"

Patience looked up to see Shirley sticking her head into her office. Was lunch over already? Automatically she glanced at her watch. Five after two. Time to get back to work, she thought, rising from her desk.

She crumbled the foil around her uneaten, almost untouched tuna fish sandwich, sending both unceremoniously into the wastepaper basket. By her reckoning, she had to have lost two pounds in the last two days. Her appetite had completely disappeared. Maybe she was onto something, she mocked herself. She could call it the lovesick diet.

Except that she wasn't lovesick, she insisted silently. Just a little love-under-the-weather.

She pasted a smile on her face as she turned toward her receptionist. "I'm coming, Shirley." She began to circumvent the desk. "Who's up first?"

Shirley glanced over her shoulder, as if her memory wasn't sufficient to retain that kind of information for more than a few moments at a time. "That man who came with that bird."

Instantly, Patience tensed. The hairs on the back of her neck began to stand up like some elementary science experiment involving a glass rod and a swatch of fur. She'd distinctly told Shirley to turn him away if he called for an appointment. Had he just shown up again?

"Walter Payne?"

Shirley's head bobbed up and down. The woman's eyes watched her anxiously. "Um, I think so."

She couldn't deal with this, not right now. Not when she felt so terribly scattered. "Tell him I'm too busy. Give him Dr. Johnson's number."

"But he's already here," Shirley told her. "In the office—."

Patience squared her shoulders. "Don't argue with me, Shirley. I said—"

She stopped abruptly as a shadow fell across Shirley. Walter stood on the threshold, a square white box in his hands. Without thinking, Patience opened the middle drawer of her desk. Her hand covered the scissors she kept there.

"I won't take any of your time," Walter promised her. "I just came by to give you this present. It's to say thank-you. Mitzi's doing fine."

"Paying your bill says thank-you, Walter," she replied crisply. Her heart hammered hard as she closed her fingers around the scissors.

"I wanted to settle that up, too. I won't be here to get your bill, Dr. Cavanaugh. Mitzi and I are moving away."

Was he telling her this to throw her off? Or was he finally giving up? Her emotions were in such a state of turmoil, she didn't know what to think. And she was afraid to hope.

"When?"

"At the end of this week." Taking a couple of steps forward, Walter slipped the box onto her desk. "We're going down to San Diego. Weather's better for Mitzi and I've got family there. My brother just got laid off and he thought it might be a good time to start something new. He's going to be joining me in my company." Walter's expression took on a forlorn look. "So you see, this is kind of like a good-bye present."

"I still can't accept it. That would be unprofessional," she added in the hope that the words would finally convince him. But Walter made no move to take back his gift. Or to leave. "All right, then, goodbye." Why wasn't he going?

He looked at her hopefully, ignoring the fact that Shirley still stood there, seeming befuddled. "Of course, with the Internet and all, we could still stay in touch if you'd like—"

Patience cut him off. "I don't think that's a good idea, Walter."

"But if Mitzi gets sick again—"

"There are a great many good vets down in San Diego."

"Right." Walter sighed, crestfallen. "Well, then, I guess I'd better get going." Picking up the gift, he paused by the doorway. "Thanks again for all your help. Mitzi will never forget you."

"And I certainly won't forget Mitzi," she murmured under her breath.

"One more thing—" he began.

"Walter, I think you really need to go now." She squared her shoulders, moving out of her office. Forcing him to step back.

"Everything all right here?"

Startled, Patience turned to find Josh standing with Gonzo in the small hallway.

Finding himself so close to the dog, Walter's eyes nearly bulged. He cringed, pressing himself against the wall in an effort to vacate the confining area without making contact with the animal. He never took his eyes off Gonzo until he'd cleared the hall.

"It is now," Patience told Josh. She tried to keep the relief out of her voice, but doubted if she succeeded.

Chapter 12

Josh glanced over his shoulder at Walter's disappearing figure. Shirley muttered something about answering the phone and slipped away.

"Did I just miss something?" Josh's eyes narrowed as he looked back at her.

"No." She didn't feel like going into a long story. Instead, Patience looked at the large German shepherd standing behind Josh in the limited space. "What can I do for you?"

He didn't answer immediately. Instead Josh watched her for a long moment, then smiled. "Well, since you asked…"

Because the game was familiar and because he'd shown up at precisely the right time, she flashed him an amused smile. "I was referring to Gonzo."

"Can't blame a guy for trying." Josh shrugged, as if resigned to making the best of it. "Well, as it turns out, I forgot to ask you for Gonzo's heartworm medication. He ran out."

Walking to where the files were all kept in the passageway, Patience paused a moment to look for Gonzo's. Finding it, she pulled it out, then turned to the last entry as she entered the closest exam room.

"That's odd." She flipped through several pages before looking up at Josh. "According to this, he should have enough to last him through the beginning of next month."

Josh's expression bordered on the sheepish. "That's provided he didn't let one of the pills go rolling down the sink."

She closed the file and looked at Josh, puzzled. "You're going to have to elaborate on that."

Josh leaned a hip against the examination table. "I tossed it to him because that's the way he likes to take pills." She gave him an incredulous look. "Trying to shove them down his throat doesn't work," he explained. "Anyway, I tossed, he jumped, the damn thing bounced off his nose and landed in the sink, where it went down the drain, making us one pill short."

Patience shook her head and laughed. "So, you think you're Michael Jordan, do you?" She petted Gonzo's head, then turned toward the cabinet where she kept certain standard medications. The one she was looking for came prepackaged in a six-month supply. Finding it, she handed the small box to Josh. "Here, this should hold him for the next six months. And you might just try giving it to him instead of having him field it."

Josh pocketed the box. "He doesn't like swallowing pills the regular way."

She ran her hand along the dog's well-brushed coat. "He does when I give it to him."

Josh laughed shortly, as if what she'd just said was self-evident. "Gonzo would probably stand still for an enema if you were the one giving it to him."

Patience cocked her head as she looked at Gonzo's partner. A bemused smile curved her lips. "That has got to be the strangest compliment I ever got, but thank you—I think."

The reason for the unexpected visit concluded, Josh appeared reluctant to leave. He nodded toward the back office. "What was going on here when I came in? You seemed…threatened."

So much for keeping a poker face, she thought. "Did I?"

Patience blew out a breath, debating. She'd thought that Brady had told Josh earlier about Walter. But maybe he hadn't. It seemed that her ability to read Brady came up short. In a lot of ways.

Since he'd pushed, she gave Josh a quick summary, without the highlights. The less she said about the situation, the faster she could put it behind her. "For some reason, Walter Payne got it into his head that there might be something between us if he just pressed hard enough."

By his expression, this was obviously news to Josh. She saw anger crease his forehead just before he nodded toward the outer door. "That little weasel?"

"He's not a weasel, he's just—" She shrugged, searching for the right word, and then settled on "—misguided. And lonely."

Josh's eyes grew dark. "Did he try anything?"

A vein popped up on Josh's brow. Signs of a temper she'd never been aware of became evident. Patience placed her hands on his chest, as if that could hold him down. "Whoa, Captain America, hold it, it's okay," she teased. "Walter just came by to tell me goodbye. He's moving."

Josh appeared unconvinced. "I can keep an eye on him for you."

She shook her head. "Not necessary."

But Josh didn't seem to think she was right. "Maybe a woman like you doesn't realize what kind of fatal attraction she represents."

She knew that she didn't stop clocks when she passed, but she'd never thought of herself as particularly beautiful, either. "I'd hardly call it fatal."

"That's because you're oblivious to it. But other

people aren't." There was a glimmer of annoyance in his voice. "Like Coltrane."

The mention of the man who had disappeared from her life brought with it a strange feeling that rippled through her. She felt oddly abandoned, even though she'd tried, over and over, to talk herself out of it. Coming from the family that she did, she knew all the reasons that could have kept Brady from coming to see her. Policemen didn't exactly keep regular hours. But that shouldn't have stopped Brady from at least giving her a two-second phone call just to touch base. To…

What was she doing? She didn't want this relationship, so why was she pining?

Because she was going crazy, that's why.

Patience brushed back a strand of hair that had come undone from the clip at the back of her neck. "Could we change the subject?"

"Fine with me." The smile on Josh's lips was warm and sensuously teasing. "Let's talk about something closer to home."

"Like Gonzo."

His eyes held hers. "I was thinking of something a little more human."

"You're insulting him." She grinned, petting the dog again. Gonzo seemed to curl into her touch. She gave him one final pat and picked up his chart again, heading for the door. "And now that you have his pills, I'd better get back to my other patients or I'm liable to be here all night.''

Josh walked out the door with her. "Call me the next time you need rescuing."

She laughed. "I will."

He paused before going into the reception area. "I mean it."

He sounded so serious. Had he seen something in Walter Payne's eyes that she'd missed? No, she couldn't let herself think that way. She wasn't going to live her life glancing over her shoulder all the time. It was time to end this conversation.

Patience looked down at the German shepherd. "Gonzo, be a good dog and take your master back to work."

Gonzo barked once, as if in agreement, and then led Josh out. The latter gave her a quick wink before he allowed himself to be dragged off.

She shook her head and laughed as she entered the next exam room.

It had been a very long day, with two emergencies that had to be wedged into her appointments. An undersize cocker spaniel had had an altercation with a rosebush and lost; and a Great Dane had decided to help herself to some chocolate cake that had been left out on the dining room table. Luckily the dog's owner had stopped her before she'd consumed the whole thing. Chocolate could often be deadly for a dog.

Lucky the same wasn't true for humans, Patience thought, locking the door. Tonight's main course was going to be a pint of chocolate ice cream. She had no desire to make anything edible on her own and didn't even feel like putting out the energy to dial a number for take-out.

Claiming to be coming down with a cold, Shirley had long since gone home, leaving her to juggle patients, charts and payment statements on her own. Exhausted, Patience was about to shut off the lights when she heard pounding on the door.

Everything inside her froze.

Was that Walter?

Lulling her into thinking he was moving away, had he decided to sneak back to see her?

She tried to calm herself down. Walter wouldn't be pounding on the door like that. That was drawing attention, not sneaking.

"Patience? Patience, are you still in there? Open the damn door!"

Brady.

Her heart resumed beating. Pounding in time to the fist that was meeting the door. Why was he yelling like that?

Patience ran to the door before the rest of her questions could even form.

The second she unlocked the door, it flew open,

banging on the opposite wall. Brady staggered in, struggling with the weight in his arms. He was carrying King. The dog was covered with blood.

Patience stifled the gasp that rose in her throat. There was no time to react as a person, only as a veterinarian. Her feelings needed to be put on hold.

"Oh my God, what happened?" Even as she asked, she was leading Brady and King back to the operating room.

In an effort to remain calm, Brady recited the events in a clipped manner. "We found a cache of drugs in a toy warehouse earlier this evening. The drugs were packed inside the dolls. They were using heroin instead of stuffing. Drug dealer had a pit bull on the premises. It went for me and King tried to save me." And then the cold act folded as his voice throbbed with emotion. "You've got to save him."

She blinked away the tears that filled her eyes. The kind of pit bull a drug dealer would have was bred to kill, and there was no more effective killing machine on the face of the planet. By scientific calculations, the jaws of a pit bull could exude over two thousand pounds of pressure when clamped.

"You could have been killed. You both could have." She pulled down a fresh sheet of exam paper to cover the table for King. "Put him on the table. How did you—"

"Get away?" he guessed. "Easy." His expression was grim. "Gillespie shot him," he told her, mentioning another patrolman assigned to the detail. He swallowed, battling fears as he looked at his long-time friend and companion. "Is he going to be all right?"

"Yes."

Her response was automatic. It was what they both needed to hear, whether or not it was logically true. She didn't want to think about odds, or possibilities, or what could go wrong. Nothing was going to go wrong. She was going to *make* the dog be all right.

"Hold him down for a second," she instructed. Then, while Brady did so, she prepared a syringe, tapping the side to make sure there was no air bubble trapped inside

"What's that?" Brady immediately demanded.

"Just a sedative to make him relax." She nodded toward the reception area. "Why don't you wait for me outside?"

His feet firmly planted on the ground, Brady made no move to go. "No."

She slipped on the blue operating gown and prepared a tray. "It's going to get messy."

She could argue until she was blue in the face, nothing short of an order from God was going to get him to leave. And maybe not even then. "He's my dog. I'm staying."

She didn't have the time to waste arguing. The

dog needed her now and needed her focused. "Okay, then stay out of my way."

Patience washed her hands, then quickly pulled on a pair of rubber gloves before beginning her examination. The dog, mercifully, was already asleep.

Both of King's ears had been bitten, and a piece was missing from the tip of one. But the wounds she was more concerned about were the ones along the canine's throat. There were a total of three separate tears. It was obvious that the pit bull had intended to rip out King's throat.

But when she examined them, she saw that the tears were superficial. She looked up at Brady. He was like a stone statue, standing guard. It reminded her of an old fairy tale Patrick had read to her. *The Steadfast Tin Soldier.* "How did you manage to keep the dog from ripping King's throat apart?"

"I pushed them together." His arms ached just to think about the ordeal. He'd used every last bit of strength he had and then some to hold the pit bull against King. Otherwise, the dog would have bitten through chunks of King's throat.

"Quick thinking." If Brady hadn't been quick, there was no question in her mind that King would have been dead in moments.

"If I'd been quick, I would have shot him myself before he got to King."

Though sedated, the dog twitched slightly as she

cleaned off his wounds. She started to repair the damage. "But the pit bull got to you first, right?"

"Yeah."

Patience glanced up at him from her suturing. Brady's shirt was covered with blood. She nodded at it. "How much of that is yours?"

He looked down to see what she was talking about. He'd been running on empty ever since he'd seen the untethered dog come at them. After the attacking dog had been taken down, Gillespie had offered to drive him to an all night vet's, but he'd refused. Refused to allow anyone to touch him or his dog. He'd wanted to come to her. Because he was afraid that if he didn't, no one else could save King.

He was still afraid.

"I don't know."

"Why don't you let me help—"

He didn't even let her finish. "After you sew up King," he ordered.

Patience knew without being told that there was no reasoning with him. In a way, she supposed she understood. She would have placed Tacoma's well-being before her own.

"Okay," she agreed.

It was more than an hour before Patience finally stripped off her gloves and operating gown. She'd done all she could for the dog, the rest was out of her hands, but she felt pretty confident that all had gone well.

They moved King onto a pallet in the corner of the room. The dog was still sedated, but beginning to come around. "He needs to rest now," she told Brady.

He nodded. "I'm going to stay here." He began to pull up a chair.

"First we're going to see just how much of that blood was yours, remember? Take your shirt off."

He waved her away. He'd sustained worse at his father's hands when he was a kid. "I'm okay."

Her eyes narrowed. "The hell you are." Not waiting for him to comply, Patience picked up a pair of surgical scissors and began to cut his bloody shirt away from his body.

He knew better than to jerk away. "Hey, what are you doing?"

"Taking matters into my own hands." Brady started to stop her, only to have his hand pushed away. "Sit down," she ordered. When he didn't, she warned, "Don't mess with me, Coltrane." Her eyes blazed. All the feelings surrounding this man suddenly came rushing up from inside her. It was almost too much for her to deal with at one time. "You don't want to see me when I'm angry."

Brady did as he was ordered and sat on the examination table. Despite himself, he was amused. "Didn't the Hulk say something like that?"

She spared him a look that told him he'd better not be laughing at her. "The Hulk didn't talk. That was his alter ego and right now, I'd say it was pretty good advice."

His stomach tightened reflexively as she dabbed peroxide on the first of his wounds. It took him a second to find his breath. "Why are you angry?"

Ordinarily she would have shrugged away his question and kept everything inside. But he was hurt and bleeding and he might have been killed today, leaving her with all these unresolved feelings that had nowhere to go. Damn it, she wasn't supposed to care like this. "Because it takes King and you almost bleeding to death to get you to show up," she said, her voice vibrating with anger.

"I'm not bleeding to death—"

She shot him a dark look. "Don't twist my words around, Coltrane. You're in a very dangerous spot right now."

He looked at the scissors on the examination table beside him. "Yeah, I know." And then, because the look in her eyes had gotten to him, he decided that, for once in his life, he was going to tackle something other than stone-cold facts. "Look, I thought it was for the best if I left you alone."

Patience finished cleaning another wound. Tossing away the swab, she turned her attention to the third. "Whose best?"

"Yours." The answer was automatic, without thought. And then he added, "Maybe mine."

"Why?" Very delicately, she applied a salve to the wound. She could see his skin tighten.

"Because you said you didn't want to get involved with a cop."

She raised her eyes to his. "I think we've passed the 'get' part and are well into 'involved,' wouldn't you say?"

Brady swallowed a curse born more of frustration than of the physical pain he was experiencing. "Patience, I don't know the first thing about being in a relationship."

She examined her work before continuing on to the next wound. He was lucky the pit bull hadn't turned him into a human chew toy.

"They're a little like snowflakes, every one is just a little bit different from the rest." She looked at him again. "You go from there."

She didn't get it yet, did she? He had no frame of reference to fall back on, nothing to guide him as to what he should do, what he should feel. "I grew up in a house full of anger and hate."

"The man who put himself between his dog and a pit bull knows more than just anger and hate. He knows about love and sacrifice." There were three more wounds, all in a row along his rib cage. She liberally applied peroxide to all three and winced along with him. "Look, I'm scared, too. Maybe we can be scared together."

She felt him backing away from her. "I didn't say I was scared."

The right corner of her mouth rose slightly. "You didn't have to." Taking a fresh swab, she wiped away the blood from his forehead. Studying it, she frowned. Brady had a gash there that was going to form a nasty scar if it wasn't sutured.

"Finished?" he asked impatiently.

"Almost. You've got a nasty cut right above your eyebrow. I'm going to have to stitch that up."

He looked at her dubiously. Left on his own, he would have just washed the wound and left it alone. "Are you qualified to do that?"

She went to get a new suturing tray. "Yes, I'm qualified to do that."

He shifted, uncomfortable. He didn't like being fussed over. "I won't start having cravings for dog biscuits after you finish, will I?"

"No." She brought the tray over to the table. "But you might have this urge to bay at a full moon every once in a while."

He thought of the way he'd felt, making love with her. "I had that urge the other night."

Patience took the cellophane off the tray, aware that he was watching her every move. She tossed the cellophane into the wastepaper basket. "Then this shouldn't be a problem for you."

No, he thought, but being so close to her was. Because, despite the aches that began to take hold of him, he could feel himself responding to her. Could feel himself wanting her. This was far too intimate a setting for them to be alone together.

He watched her thread a needle. "You don't have to do this."

The look she gave him told him to stop arguing with her. "Yes, I do."

Brady began to slide off the table. "I could go to a hospital."

She put her hand in the middle of his chest and pushed. She was surprisingly strong for such a little thing. "But you won't."

He knew he could easily overpower her. All he had to do was to get off the table and just keep walking. But he wanted to remain near King. And to do that, he had to let Patience do what she wanted to.

Brady frowned. "I don't think I like having you be able to read me so well."

She looked at him and said, "Tough," before she went back to work.

The single word echoed, inching its way along a wireless path out into the night. Taken there by the electronic devices that had been covertly placed throughout the clinic and her house. The devices she knew nothing about.

The devices her stalker had planted.

Chapter 13

Brady sat amazingly still as she sutured the gash on his forehead. Not a muscle moved when she pushed the needle through his skin. Each time she took another stitch she could almost feel the needle breaking the surface. Yet he gave no indication that he felt anything at all. Maybe he was channeling his pain, she mused.

"There," she announced, completing the last stitch. "Done. You're free to go."

About to put on his shirt, he glanced at the shredded garment then left it where it was. Between the pit bull's attack and Patience's pass with her scissors, there was no saving the shirt. He reached for his jacket instead, then looked over toward where his dog was sleeping on the pallet on the floor. "How long is he going to be like that?"

Patience glanced at her watch, gauging the amount of anesthetic she'd given the animal. "King should be waking up in a few hours. There's nothing more you can do for him right now, so if you want to go home—"

"I don't want to go home."

He was looking at her, not King, when he said it. She felt her flesh warming. It took her a minute to find her tongue. With effort, she picked up the tray she'd just used and set aside the instruments.

"I've got a spare bed in the guest room I can make up for you upstairs."

"I don't want to be in the guest room."

Very slowly, she turned around to gaze at him. All her pulses were suddenly awake and active. Her anticipation was at a heightened level. "Then what is it you do want?"

He touched her face and felt that same longing spring up within him he'd felt before. The longing that only seemed to be associated with her. The longing he'd never felt before.

"You."

"I see."

It was as if everything inside her had been holding its breath. And now she felt herself melting. Logic tried desperately to break through the barriers she'd set up. She was getting in too deep and the deeper she went, the less chance she had of coming back out again. At least, not whole.

But logic stood very little chance of succeeding tonight. It found itself pitted against a very particular reality. She could have easily lost Brady today. Lost him to a bullet or a pit bull or God only knew what else. Lost him to all the pitfalls that were out there, waiting to take out a man who wore a badge and strapped on a gun each morning. But she realized that rather than run from what she found here, in his arms, she was going to make the most of it. For as long as she had. And if that was just for tonight, okay. If it was for longer, well then, even better.

But she knew she couldn't count on anything beyond the moment she was in. Being a policeman's daughter had taught her that. And she had always been one to make the most of what she had.

Patience smiled up into his face. "Shouldn't be a difficult prescription to fill." She moved closer to him until she was in his arms. "Are you sure you won't hurt too much?"

What was too much? He was already aching. Mostly for her. Very slowly he moved his head from side to side, giving Patience her answer. "I'd hurt even more if I went home."

Her smile widened. "You know, for a man who doesn't talk all that much, you do come up with some lovely things to say."

"Must be the company I'm keeping."

She laughed softly, touching his face. How had she gotten here? And how had she managed to resist for so long? "I'll accept that."

Brady bent his head and kissed her. And everything else faded away. The concerns, the pain, and most of all the loneliness that ached so badly it threatened to swallow him up whole and send his soul back to the abyss from where it had come. He had no idea how he had managed to stay away from her for these past two days. Nor could he remember why.

An urgency filled her, making her want to race even as she wanted to savor every tiny moment, absorbing it like a sponge. Even as his mouth slanted over hers, taking her higher and higher into the euphoria that he created for them, she was fumbling with his belt, desperate to undress him. Desperate to make love with him.

She managed to unnotch his gun belt. Heavy, it slid down the length of his legs like a lead weight, thudding to the floor in a semicircle around his feet. She didn't wait for the sound to register before she started to undo the belt on his pants.

Her heart vibrated like a tuning fork as she pushed the button through its hole and then pulled down the zipper. She bit back a moan of anticipation as, his kiss deepening, he ripped away buttons on her shirt, yanking away the material.

And then touching her.

Softly, reverently, in complete conflict with the wild, erotic sensations that slammed through her like an ocean of tiny rubber balls.

She wanted him to take her this second. She grasped his shoulders to anchor herself to him as her knees began to feel as if they were buckling. When he winced in response, guilt filled her.

She pulled back to look at him. "You're sure I'm not hurting you."

Pain was the last thing on his mind. And she was the first.

"Woman, you talk too much." His voice was thick with desire.

The next moment Brady was covering her mouth with his own again, kissing her if his very soul hung in the balance.

And then she couldn't talk, couldn't muster up the concern she'd felt only a second ago, because he was assaulting every square inch of her, both literally and figuratively.

Scrambling for more and more sensations, they discarded the rest of each other's clothing. Within moments, with internal flames urging them on, they were on the floor, wrapped up in one another.

She found she could hardly breathe. Brady had her completely on fire. The first time had been perfect. But it paled in comparison to now. She didn't know where to touch first, what to feel first. Everything was exquisitely delicious. Every vital part of

her throbbed, waited for release, wanted him forever. She twisted and turned as he caressed her over
and over again. His body was hard and firm and she
couldn't get enough of him.

When he finally drove himself into her, their
hands locked together, their bodies pressed against
one another, she bit down on her lip to keep from
crying out.

Together they raced to the final moment. When it
came, she did cry out his name. It escaped in an
exhausted whisper that echoed in his head long after
it had faded from the air.

Rather than experience the letdown that went
hand in hand with the vanishing euphoria, Brady
discovered that, inexplicably, a sweetness had begun
to fill him. He couldn't make heads or tails of it,
only knew that it was her doing.

She was some kind of a witch, casting spells over
him. Turning his life upside down. Making him
want things he had no business wanting. A home, a
family. A normal life. None of which he had any
firsthand experience with.

Using the remainder of his strength, Brady gathered her against him in his arms. Everything within
him felt as if it was smiling. His own mouth curved.

"So," he finally said, "this is your idea of a prescription."

Her body curled against his, Patience feathered
her fingertips along his chest. The light sprinkling

of hair excited her. She raised her eyes to his, hoping she looked at least a little wicked, because he made her feel very, very wicked.

"Uh-huh."

Didn't she know how impossible this was? How could she when he was acting as if it was the most normal thing in the world? As if making love to an angel was an everyday occurrence for him instead of a miracle.

He ran his thumb along her lower lip. Exciting himself. "When can I come by for another refill?"

"Anytime you want."

"Good to know." Brady sucked his breath in sharply as he felt her fingers lightly glide along his inner thigh, then delve farther down. He placed his hand over hers as she cupped him.

Her grin was positively wicked. "Now might be a good time."

Her breath was warm along his chest. One minute he was exhausted; the next, he wanted her again. Patience was teaching him things about himself he'd never known before.

Brady rolled over onto her again. "Sounds good to me."

The agony was overwhelming.

He couldn't make himself leave.

Like a penitent sinner, bent on self-torture, he remained throughout the night, caught in his own private hell as he listened to the sounds.

The sounds of their making love.

Anger had long since taken hold of him, sharing a dance with a red-hot jealousy that gave him no peace.

Would give him no peace until he acted.

The first time had been a mistake. But he could find no way to absolve her of the second time. That was just wrong. She'd transgressed.

It was time.

Time to make her realize that she belonged to him and only him, not this sanctimonious jackass in a uniform.

His fists clenched at his sides.

It was time.

Brady stayed the night. He'd had no intentions of staying, at least, not in her bed, but it seemed as if his intentions made no impression on the plans life had laid down for him. He'd been fooling himself all these years, he thought as he pulled on his jacket, by believing that he was in charge of his own destiny. He wasn't.

Not in the absolute sense.

He knew he could still walk away from Patience, and he still believed, deep in his soul, that it would be for her own good if he did. But he also knew that if he did so, he would be leaving a piece of himself behind. A piece he hadn't even known he'd had until recently.

Leaving her would cost him his heart.

"When can I take King home?" he asked. They were in her kitchen and he'd just turned down her offer to make him breakfast. He shook his head when she held the coffeepot over his cup. He'd already had three cups and, for now, that was his limit.

She set the pot down on her side. Something was in the air. She felt too antsy herself to eat. "I'd like to keep him here for a few more hours, now that he's awake. Just to make sure."

Make sure of what? he wondered. Half-formed thoughts filled his head. "You think he's in any danger?"

"No." *Not nearly as much as I am,* she added silently. Because Brady had her heart and she was vulnerable now. Just the way she'd always sworn to herself she would never be.

So much for keeping promises made to yourself.

An awkwardness had descended over them. It had been there from the moment they'd stepped into the kitchen. From the moment they'd stepped into the rest of their lives outside of her bedroom. "Well, I guess I'd better report in."

She didn't want him to leave, didn't want last night to end, even though daylight had pushed itself into every corner of her house.

"Can't you take the day off?" She glanced down

at the floor, toward where the clinic's back room
was one floor away. "After all, your partner's re-
cuperating—and so should you."

He looked at her for a long moment, feeling so
many things he didn't want to feel. Things he had
no idea how to handle. This simple woman who
asked for nothing had turned his whole world upside
down and made everything come spilling out. How
was he supposed to get it all back together again?

"This is going to take more time than just a day
to get over."

She could feel an ominous cloud descending,
"You're not talking about your wounds, are you?"

"No," he told her quietly.

She took her courage into both her hands. Anything worth having was worth fighting for, she'd
once heard. And Brady was so worth having. "Do
you really think this is something you need to get
over?"

No, if he was lucky, he'd remember every single
moment he'd spent with her forever. But that wasn't
the point. "No, but you need me to get over it."

"Coltrane, get this through your head. I do not
need anyone else doing my thinking for me, or de-
ciding what's best for me."

Her fierce declaration left him unmoved. "Maybe
in this case, you do."

"No," she replied firmly, quietly. So quietly she
could hear her heart cracking. "I don't. But you

obviously need some time.'' She rose from the table, picking up his empty cup and hers. Had King not been in her recovery area, she would have taken Brady over to her uncle's for breakfast and maybe that would have done the trick for him.

But then, if King hadn't been hurt, Brady might not have been here in the first place.

Patience sighed. She ran her hand through her hair. It was still damp from the shower they had taken together. That hadn't been his plan, of course. She'd jumped into the stall after he'd already gotten started showering. His growl of surprise had turned into a guttural sound of pleasure. The shower had taken him far longer than he'd anticipated, but he'd told her he had no complaints on that account. He'd made her laugh when he'd said that for the first time in his life, his back felt as if it was completely clean.

Was that the first of many showers they'd take together?

Or was it the last?

She just didn't know. But she was determined that she wasn't about to appear needy if he decided to walk away. Pride had to come in someplace, even if it was a poor substitute for love.

Patience rose from the table. ''Like you said, you need to get to work. And so do I.''

Brady nodded as he got up. ''I just want to say goodbye to King.''

The door that led down to the clinic was already

unlocked. They'd gone to check on King together first thing this morning. Well, second thing, she amended, remembering the shower.

The thought was accompanied by a bittersweet sensation. With effort, she pulled herself back from it. "I'll let you two have a moment alone."

Brady nodded. For the time being he preferred it that way.

The morning dragged by.

Patience felt conflicted and horribly vulnerable. For the first time in a very long time, she felt as if she had little control over her emotions. They felt as if they were all over the map and it took effort to keep them from spilling out.

Damn him, anyway.

She'd been ready to throw out all of her own rules of engagement, ready to open up her heart to him completely and this morning, at the table, he'd looked as if he was ready to shut the door on it all. She could literally feel him withdrawing from her.

He'd hardly said a word after looking in on King again. Just a mumbled goodbye and that he'd be by later to pick up his partner.

And that was it.

So maybe that was it, she thought sadly. He certainly didn't behave like a man who wanted to prolong a relationship. And if she didn't want it to be over, well, obviously she had no control over the situation.

She was going to have to make her peace with that.

Peace was coming at a very high price today. Shirley had been talking almost nonstop all morning, the sound of her voice droning in the background like the overly long score to an uninteresting movie.

After a day that had been all but bursting at the seams yesterday, today the appointments were so spread out, it seemed as if the hours crawled by. She told herself she could use the rest, but right now, in her present state of mind, she wanted a day that was so busy she couldn't take two breaths together in succession.

It was on days like today that she usually took the time to catch up, but nothing was getting caught. Her brain had taken a holiday.

She was in the back office when she heard the bell jingling, announcing that someone had walked into the clinic. Good, she could use the distraction. Anything to silence her own thoughts and Shirley's incessant talking.

Coming to the reception area, she saw Josh. Gonzo was nowhere around. Taking a deep breath, she forced a smile to her lips.

The serious expression on his face made her feel uneasy. "Hi. Where's your partner?"

"At the station." His tone was somber, his words measured, as if he didn't know how to deliver them. "Patience, Brady's been hurt."

This was it, this was what she'd always feared. Her head began to ache as she tried to sort her thoughts out.

"Oh, God. How bad?" Rounding the counter, she was at his side.

Josh didn't mince words. "Bad. He's at the hospital. He asked me to come get you."

He was asking for her? That didn't sound like Brady. This had to be bad. Her heart felt constricted within her chest.

"Shirley." She tossed the name over her shoulder, not bothering to even look at the receptionist. "I'm going with Josh to the hospital to see Brady. If anyone comes in, either reschedule their appointment or, if it's urgent, send them to Dr. Johnson." As in the case of most doctors, she and the other vet covered each other's patients. "And look in on King for me."

"Will do," Shirley promised, calling after her as Patience flew out of the clinic. "Call me as soon as you know anything," she begged. But Patience was already gone.

"All right, no kid gloves. Tell me everything. What happened to Brady?" Patience demanded as she got into Josh's car.

He took off the second she closed the door.

"Some guy went nuts at the gas station on Wayne and Murphy. Said the attendant was out to get him. He pulled a gun. Brady tried to disarm him. He'd just stopped there to fill up," Josh explained. "The gun went off during the struggle."

She thought of the story that Brady had told her about attempting to wrestle the gun from his father. That had had fatal results for his father.

Was it Brady's turn now?

Her blood ran cold even as she struggled to push the thought out of her head.

Brady had felt guilty all morning. He'd left things on a bad note with Patience. It wasn't as if he'd changed his mind about his underlying concern. He knew that staying in her life would probably only result in grief for her.

But contemplating not being part of it tore him apart. It had only been a few hours since he'd made up his mind not to see her again. He'd thought, after the first time, that he could walk away. Two days of that had him crumbling. He'd found himself thinking about her almost constantly. She was like a fever of the blood and he didn't know what to do about it. The only possible antidote to the way he felt was more of the same.

Damn, was this what love was, feeling as if someone was tearing you apart and disintegrating you into tiny, useless pieces? Did it mean struggling with an overwhelming desire to see them again, to be with them again even though there was only heartache at the end of the road?

He had no answers, only questions.

And a longing so huge that he felt it was going to eat him up alive.

He lasted four hours. By the beginning of the fifth, he found himself turning his vehicle toward the familiar path that led to the clinic. Even pretending that he was just going to see King felt like a flimsy lie. He couldn't fool himself. He was going to see her.

Squaring his shoulders, Brady walked into the clinic. For once it was completely empty. He heard off-key singing coming from the back.

"Hello?" he called.

In response, Shirley popped her head around the corner. Confusion descended over her face the moment she saw him, followed by a huge, relieved smile. Shirley rushed around to the other side of the counter. "Should you be up and around?"

Obviously, Patience must have told her about the less-than-friendly encounter with the pit bull last night. He shrugged carelessly.

"Yes," he answered tersely. "Is the Doc around?"

"No, she went to see you."

Why would she leave her practice in the middle of the day? "When?"

Shirley stopped to think, then glanced at the clock on the wall. ''An hour ago.''

There hadn't been any calls from dispatch, or on his cell. ''Did she say where she was going?''

''The hospital.'' Shirley looked at him wide-eyed, as if she was examining him for bullet holes. ''That's where Josh said you were. He's the one who came to get her.''

Brady stared at her, a very sick feeling suddenly spreading through his stomach.

Chapter 14

Patience struggled to keep her imagination from running away with her. The inside of the car felt hot and stifling as she fought to get hold of herself. "How badly is Brady hurt?"

Josh spared her a look. An odd expression crossed his face. "That would upset you, wouldn't it? That he was badly hurt."

She stared at him. How could Josh even ask such a question? "Of course I'd be upset. I *am* upset." It was difficult to keep her voice from rising. "I'd be upset if anyone I knew would be badly hurt."

What was wrong with him? she wondered, irritated. Okay, he and Brady weren't exactly friends, but this was a fellow policeman Josh was talking about. There was supposed to be a bond between them, a loyalty that went beyond petty issues.

Stepping on the gas, Josh drove right through a light that was turning red. She saw his hands tighten on the wheel. Maybe Brady was dead and he was searching for a way to tell her.

Oh, dear God, don't let him be dead. Please don't let him be dead.

Josh slanted a look at her before focusing back on the flow of traffic. "But this is special, isn't it, Patience? You'd *really* be upset if Brady was hurt."

Something didn't feel right, and anxiety began to undulate through her.

"What do you mean, 'if'? Is Brady hurt or not?" she asked. Josh made no answer. They whizzed through traffic, switching from lane to lane. She braced her hand against the dashboard as he took a right corner. "Josh, what's going on here?"

She saw his face darken, his jaw clench. A malevolence hardened in his eyes as he turned toward her. "Don't take that high-handed tone with me, you little liar."

Patience stared at him, stunned. The word was a slap in the face. What the hell was going on with him? He'd always been so easygoing, so charming. Had something happened on the job to make him crack?

"Liar?"

He snorted contemptuously. "What would you

call it? You go on and on about your precious rules. Rules for this, rules for that,'' he mimicked her voice. ''Rules for not getting involved with a policeman.'' The singsong tone stopped. Pure rage vibrated in his tone. ''Those rules didn't stop you from getting involved with Coltrane, did they?''

She stiffened. How did he know? ''What are you talking about? I'm not involved with Coltrane.''

''Stop lying to me,'' he shouted. The veins along his neck bulged, his face turning a deep shade of red. ''You think I don't know? That I'm stupid or something? Is that it? You think I don't know that you've been sleeping with him?''

The noises within the vehicle blended and faded into the background. She could hear the blood rushing in her veins. ''And how would you know that?''

He took another sharp turn. She struggled not to lean into him.

''Because I know everything there is to know about you, Patience. I know all about your family, about how your father mistreated your mother and that's why you're afraid to go out with a policeman. I know that you're wasting your time with someone like Coltrane when I'm the one who understands you. I'm the one who can love you the way you deserve to be loved.'' The cell phone rang in her purse. He glared at it accusingly. ''Don't answer that.''

Her heart raced. Josh was acting crazy. She

needed to get away before his reckless driving killed them both.

"But it could be about a patient," she protested.

He knew better. "And it could be Coltrane, looking for you. Don't answer that!" It wasn't a warning but a threat. Josh put out his hand. "Give me your cell," he ordered.

Patience opened her purse. Damn it, why wasn't she one of those women who carried everything but the kitchen sink in her purse? If she had scissors, a screwdriver or even a sharpened pencil, she could have used it on him. But her purse was the very essences of barren. She had nothing there to use as a weapon. Taking out her phone, she placed it in his hand.

The sinking feeling in the pit of her stomach nauseated her. Josh was the one, not Walter. For one insane second, she'd even thought it might have been Shirley wanting to make her think someone was interested in her so that her attention would be drawn away from Brady. But it was neither of them. It had been Josh all along.

"You sent the flowers, didn't you?" The words echoed within the car.

She saw his shoulders stiffen. He shot her an accusing look. "I would have sent you an ocean of roses if you'd just stopped lying and gone out with me." His face contoured into a sneer. "But you didn't even want to give me a chance. Just Coltrane."

"It's not like that."

"Isn't it?" he demanded hotly. "You didn't take him into your bed last night? Didn't shower with him this morning?"

The accusations, so on target, stole her breath away. She could feel the skin along her arms and neck puckering into gooseflesh. There was only one way he could have been so dead-on.

"You have the house bugged."

His sneer only deepened. "Only way to find out what you're up to."

Patience pressed her lips together. Her stomach rose up into her throat. She fought not to throw up.

And then it hit her. She was being kidnapped. "Brady isn't in the hospital, is he?"

The laugh was dry, mocking. Cold. "If he were, I wouldn't be taking you to him."

Her mind began to scramble, searching for a way out. "Where are we going?"

When he looked at her again, his face had softened once more. It was as if two separate individuals took turns channeling through him. And she was afraid of both of them.

"Where I can talk some sense into you and make you see that we belong together."

She tried to focus on what he was like whenever he came by the clinic. Patience put her hand on his arm, making a connection, mutely supplicating. "Josh, you need help."

"No." He yanked his arm away. "I don't. I finally know what to do and how to get you to stop throwing yourself away on Coltrane. He's a murderer, you know." He let the words sink in, taking their effect. "He killed his old man."

If he expected her to be repelled, he was going to be disappointed, she thought. The threat Josh posed far outweighed anything he had to tell her about Brady. "That was an accident."

"Yeah, right." Josh laughed coldly. "That was what Coltrane wanted you to believe. It was a small hick town and the only witnesses to the murder were his mother and sister. What did you expect them to say?" They drove down a street that was unfamiliar to her. Where was he taking her? "That he did it? He was the only male member of the family left and they needed him to take care of them, of course they were going to say it was an accident."

Josh shrugged and continued, "Doesn't matter. From what I heard, the old man deserved killing. But that doesn't change what Coltrane is." He went through a red light. To her right, a car came to a screeching halt, fishtailing in a wild effort to keep from hitting them. "He's no good for you, Patience."

She summoned her most authoritative voice. She

had to get him to listen to her. "Take me home, Josh."

He didn't bother taking his eyes off the road. "I am."

And then it hit her. He was taking her to his house. To keep her a prisoner. She struggled against panic taking hold. "*My* home."

"It is," he informed her, his voice matter-of-fact. "From now on."

They drove far above the speed limit, but she felt she had only one chance to escape. Bracing herself, Patience released her seat belt, one hand on the lever of the passenger door. She heard the unmistakable click of a hammer being cocked.

"I wouldn't do that if I were you," he told her evenly. "You'd be dead before you hit the ground."

Shifting her eyes slowly, she saw the gun that he had on his lap. The gun that was now pointed at her stomach. She galvanized herself against the fear that spread through her like a forest fire.

"You won't shoot me."

"Don't go betting the farm on that. Or better yet, your life." Sarcasm dripped from every syllable. "I never was a generous man, Patience. If I can't have you, neither can Coltrane. Or anybody else." His eyes bore into her for a split second, making her blood run cold. She knew he wasn't bluffing. "Now get your damn hand off the damn door."

She did as he told her.

* * *

"I said I need his address, Woodrow. *Now*,"
Brady barked at the dispatcher on the other end of
the two-way radio. He heard nothing for a second,
then the woman rattled off Josh's address. The patrolman lived in a second-floor walk-up on the other
side of town.

"What's this all about, Officer Coltrane?" the
dispatcher asked.

He prayed he was jumping to conclusions. "I'll
fill you in when I figure it all out."

Switching on his siren, Brady tore across the city
streets. Weaving in and out of the moderate midday
traffic, he got there in record time. His vehicle had
barely stopped moving as he jumped out. Taking the
stairs two at a time, he got to the door in less than
half a minute. It was a cool morning. Brady was
perspiring so badly, his shirt stuck to his back beneath his jacket.

He hadn't been able to get hold of Josh, not
through the dispatcher, and Josh wasn't answering
his cell. Neither had Patience when he'd tried her
number. He'd let it ring for the full count, then listened as the singsong voice told him that she was
either out of range or not answering her phone.

A sense of urgency tightened around his chest like
an iron band. Brady didn't like thinking what he was
thinking.

The door to Josh's apartment was locked, but

locks had never posed an obstacle to him. He was inside in less than thirty seconds. Though it was hardly past one o'clock and sunny outside, the apartment was shrouded in darkness. The rooms were positioned so that neither the morning nor afternoon sun reached it. A gloom pervaded the area.

Unholstering his service revolver, Brady entered the small, one-bedroom apartment. There was a dankness in the air, as if windows were never opened. As if nothing from the outside world was allowed to enter here.

He moved cautiously, calling out Graham's name. There was no response. Everything inside him urged him on quickly.

It took less than five minutes to secure the apartment. Neither Josh nor Patience was here.

The Spartan bedroom had little in the way of furniture. A bed, a nightstand and a battered bureau. When he turned around to leave, the very air in his lungs froze. The wall opposite the bed was entirely devoted to Patience. There were more than a hundred different photographs of her, all candid, all taken at either the clinic or inside her house.

She didn't appear to be aware of the camera in any of the shots.

Which meant that there had to be hidden cameras, hidden eyes watching her. Cameras in her clinic. In her home. Recording the most personal of details, the most intimate of moments. There was a twenty-seven-inch television set on one side of the bed with a VCR hooked. Pressing the eject button, Brady saw a tape emerge out of the machine. He pushed it back, turned on the set and played the tape.

On the screen, he saw Patience getting ready for bed.

Brady felt sick to his stomach.

Josh was her stalker.

Hurrying out of the bedroom, his mind in a hundred different places, Brady bumped into the coffee table, smashing his shin and sending a pristine white photo album crashing facedown on the floor. The two sides spread out like a penitent sinner in front of an altar.

Brady stared at it. He didn't dare breathe as he stooped to pick it up.

Flipping the book over, he found himself looking down at an array of photographs. Page after page of photographs of Patience with Josh.

He didn't understand. Had they had a relationship? Were they involved?

No, something didn't feel right. Patience would have said something to him; he knew she would have. And Josh…Josh would have warned him off, saying something about poaching on another man's property, if there'd been a relationship. It was the kind of possessive comment Josh was prone to.

Slowly, Brady turned one page after another. Josh and Patience were on every page. Together. Exotic locales were in the background, like pictures taken of people on a vacation.

Or on a honeymoon. What the hell was going on here?

Toward the end of the album, he found several photographs of Patience and Josh taken with two children. A boy and a girl who looked like younger versions of them. That was when he realized what he was looking at. Josh's fantasy book.

One of the patrolmen at the precinct was a computer enthusiast. Peter Gillespie was always showing them photographs he'd created on his computer, putting himself into shots with famous celebrities. He did it as a joke.

Brady remembered hearing Gillespie say that he could utilize the software that the department used for updating the appearance of lost children on their database and actually create what a couple's children would look like by merging their features. To prove his point, he'd merged his own features with that of a current hot movie star.

That was what Josh was doing, except that the fictitious children were supposed to represent his offspring. His and Patience's.

Brady took the album as evidence, purposely leaving behind the tape. He didn't want to use that unless it was absolutely necessary.

Damn, how could he have not seen it? Josh was the one who was obsessed with Patience, not the skinny guy with the cockatiel. The patrolman had been watching her all this time. Which meant that Josh knew that he'd spent the night with her.

And that had pushed him to act.

But where had he taken her?

Brady racked his brain, trying to think. A fragment of a sentence echoed in the recesses of his head. Something about Josh complaining that his apartment was so small, it could easily fit into a corner of his parents' house. Josh was always running his mouth off about something, never satisfied with anything in his life. Didn't Josh's parents have a house somewhere in the city? He tried to think. Josh had complained bitterly that they wouldn't let him have the place even though they spent most of their time in another house in Florida.

Leaving the apartment, Brady hurried down the stairs and out to his car. He needed to call dispatch. Someone had to know where Josh's parents lived.

The feeling that he was running out of time hovered over him.

Patience stared out of the car at the old Victorian-style house. It sat primly on a large piece of land, like a dried up woman from another era, long since past her prime, waiting for a gentleman caller. "What is this place?"

She heard a note of pride in his voice as he stopped his car at the curb. Josh sounded like a kid, showing off. "It's my parents' house. I grew up here. Like it?"

She looked at it silhouetted against the sun, its paint peeling, the roof sagging like a head that had been bowed too long. "It's very nice."

Getting out, he quickly rounded the hood and was at her door before she had a chance to get out. Her legs felt like lead.

"It's old-fashioned, and could use some work, but I figure you could do a lot with it." Opening the door on her side, he took hold of her arm and tugged her to her feet. "You could make it into a real home for us."

She tried to resist. His grasp tightened and he pulled her along with him. "Josh, I already have a home."

His face was an impassive mask. "That was part of your old life. This is your new life." Unlocking the front door, he forced her across the threshold. "As my wife."

The words crossed her tongue like sharp razors. "Your wife?"

He closed the door firmly behind them. Releasing her, he blocked her path out. "You don't think I'm going to treat you the way Coltrane does, do you? Just shack up with you and then go off whenever I want to?" His expression softened as he stroked her hair. She struggled to keep the revulsion from her face. "No, I'm going to do everything the right way.

We'll get married and make it all legal. You don't want the kids to be ashamed of us, do you?''

"Kids?'' He had everything arranged in the fantasy within his head, she thought, fighting panic. How long had this been going on? How had she remained blind to it all?

His face brightened. "Yes, our kids.'' Taking her hand, he brought it to his lips. "I've got pictures of them. I mean, they're not really pictures of our kids, not yet—but what they're going to look like when we finally have them. I want two kids. A boy and a girl. How many do you want?''

"I haven't thought about kids.''

"I think about them all the time. Our kids. Yours and mine.'' He turned suddenly, catching her off guard. She stumbled and took a step backward. He bracketed either side of her with his arms, pinning her to the wall. "I'll make you happy, Patience, I swear I will.''

She tried to push him off, but his weight was too much for her. There was no space to even raise her knee against him.

"Josh, if you want to make me happy, please let me go. I have patients to see.''

"I keep telling you, that was your old life, you're going to have to let it go. You want to tend to anyone, you tend to me. Understand?'' As he lowered his head to kiss her, she turned hers away. Instead of her lips, Josh got a mouthful of hair. "Damn it, you're willing enough to let that lowlife kiss you, why not me?''

She raised her head, anger blazing in her eyes. She clung to her anger like a life preserver. ''Because Brady doesn't threaten to make me a prisoner, that's why.''

She watched in horror as frustration and rage passed over Josh's face, turning his complexion crimson. ''You're not a prisoner, damn it. Can't you get it through your head? This is your home.''

''If it's my home, I can leave if I want to,'' she shouted back, hoping that the show of strength would intimidate him.

''No!'' he shouted into her face. ''You can't!'' His grip tightened around her wrists. He was hurting her. ''Why are you being like this? Why can't you just be happy? Why can't you love me like I love you?''

She did her best not to wince as pain shot up and down her arms. ''Josh, you're hurting me. You said you'd never hurt me.''

Josh's face contorted with barely suppressed rage. The look in his eyes frightened her. At any moment he might go off, might decide to kill her.

''And I said you were supposed to love me! Well, if you can't love me, Patience, I'm not going to let you love anyone else. Do you hear me?'' he screamed. ''Me or nobody.''

Just then, there was a crashing noise. A shower

of glass rained into the entrance through the window on the other side of the front door.

Brady, his body huddled to form a ball, came flying through the space. Hitting the floor, he rolled, his gun already drawn and extended. The next second, he leaped to his feet, the barrel of his revolver pointed at Josh.

Surprise gave way to fury. Josh swung around, shoving Patience in front of him, using her as his shield. One arm around her chest, securing her against him, the other hand holding a gun to her temple. "You shoot, you kill her. Or I do. Either way, she's dead."

Patience saw wild fury in Brady's eyes. "Let her go, Josh," he ordered.

"You'd like that, wouldn't you? So you could have her all to yourself. Well, it's not going to work that way. This bitch is mine, not yours." Still holding the gun to her temple, he pressed a kiss to her ear, then laughed as she shivered in pure loathing. "I know how to appreciate her."

Brady kept his gun trained on Josh. "How? By putting a bullet into her?"

"If I have to," he said mildly. "She'll be mine forever then." His voice changed. The rage was back. Cold and hard this time. "Put your gun down, Coltrane, or she gets one right here, right now."

Brady's heart had stopped beating. It had the moment he'd jumped to his feet and assessed the situation. There was no doubt in his mind that Josh was insane. He knew as sure as he stood there that if he put his gun down, Graham would shoot him. But more important than that, there was no guarantee that he still wouldn't kill Patience. To make her his for all eternity.

Graham was too deranged to bargain with.

He knew what he had to do. But he had never had so much on the line before and it made him afraid. Very afraid.

His eyes never left Graham. He couldn't look at Patience, couldn't allow himself to be distracted. "If I put my gun on the floor, you'll let her go?"

"Only one way to find out. Now do it!" Josh shrieked at him. "Time's running out."

Yes, Brady thought, looking at Patience's eyes, it is.

"Don't do it, Brady, he'll kill you," Patience cried.

Brady didn't answer. He knew he had only one chance to save her.

Chapter 15

His service revolver trained on Graham, Brady shifted his eyes for less than half a second to Patience. He prayed she could pick up on his signal. He needed something to cut down on the odds.

Brady met her eyes, then looked down at the floor.

"Now!"

The single word rang out with the force of cannon fire. Patience ducked her head down, away from Josh. At the same time, Brady took dead aim and fired.

A look of sheer surprise was imprinted on Josh's face for all eternity. Along with the bullet hole that was dead center in his forehead.

The patrolman slid lifelessly down to the floor, one arm still secured around Patience. The grip on her arm loosened as he hit the rug. Her heart pounding madly, she scrambled away from the body and threw herself into Brady's arms.

In the background the sounds of sirens pierced the air, coming closer.

His gun was back in its holster. There was no more need for it. The man on the ground was no longer a threat to anyone. Brady took hold of Patience's shoulders, moving her away from him. He needed to assure himself that she was in one piece, that she wasn't harmed.

"Are you all right?" he demanded, his voice cracking like a brittle twig beneath the weight of a heavy boot. His eyes scanned her from head to toe several times. She looked shaken, but in one piece. Her clothes weren't torn and there were no bruises evident. But still he asked, "Graham didn't do anything to you?"

Nothing but terrify her. Not because she was afraid of him, but because he'd made her believe that Brady had been shot. In that small space of time, she'd lived through what every policeman's wife dreaded going through. Coming face-to-face with the mortality of someone she loved dearly. The knowledge that, this time, it wasn't true, created a rush beyond belief.

She shook her head. "No, I'm fine. It's just that

he told me you were shot. That you were in the hospital, asking for me.'' Tears rose in her eyes no matter how hard she struggled to keep them back. ''I thought you were dying.''

Brady saw the tears and knew they weren't out of fear for herself. Knew that the tears were there because of him. He took her back into his arms, letting the relief come. Telling himself it was all right. She was safe and that was all that mattered.

''I'm here, Patience,'' he said softly into her hair, holding her against him, the circle of his arms creating a barrier that, for just a moment, kept the rest of the world from reaching her. ''I'm right here.''

She clung to him tightly, unable to make the fear go away. She could have lost him. Josh's scenario could have come true. The pain was just as awful as she'd imagined. The joy in realizing it wasn't true was beyond description. At that moment, she knew where her heart was and where it would always be.

With Brady.

Within minutes the house was filled with patrolmen and detectives. Voices and noise filled the air. Patience held it at bay as long as she could, clinging to Brady. Getting her bearings.

She heard someone asking Brady for his gun. She knew it was because there were strict procedures to adhere to since it had been fired.

Back to business as usual.

Except that nothing would ever be ''usual'' again.

Suddenly her brother Patrick came bursting through the sea of people around her, pushing a paramedic out of the way. His face was a road map of concern.

"I heard the call through dispatch. Are you all right?" he cried. Since the patrolman was the closest to her, Patrick looked to Brady for confirmation before Patience ever got a chance to nod her head.

Because he was so shaken, Patience began to grow calm, centering herself. She placed a hand on her older brother's shoulder.

"I'm fine. Really. Brady saved me." She couldn't make herself look at the body on the floor. "It was Josh all along. Josh was the stalker."

Brady saw relief wash over the other man's face like a tidal wave brushing against the shore. "Anything you want, man…" Patrick said to his sister's rescuer. His voice trailed off, too filled with emotion to continue.

The words were understood.

There was only one thing Brady wanted. One thing he knew he had no right to. The one thing that would make his world complete. But rather than say anything, Brady merely nodded, letting Patrick know that he understood what was being left unsaid. They were both men of few words; there was no need to spell things out.

"There's a photo album in my car you might want to enter into evidence," he told Patrick.

"Photo album?" Patrick echoed, looking from Patience to Brady.

Her mouth felt dry, as if she'd been forced to eat sand and all the granules had found their way down her throat, rubbing it raw. She took a deep breath, telling herself that it was over.

Now all she had to do was get over it, as well.

"It's an album of photographs of Josh and me." Both men looked at her curiously. "He had a copy here," she told Brady. Her eyes shifted toward her brother. "Josh used upgraded software to put us together in locations I've never been to." Unable to help herself, she shivered. "He even made up composite photographs of what our kids would look like." She swallowed and tried to find strength. "All this time and I never realized what was going on." She looked at her brother. "He didn't seem like the obsessive type."

"Those are the worst ones," Patrick told her.

Brady looked at Patience. He didn't know if she knew, if she'd figured it out yet. "He had the clinic and house bugged."

She pressed her lips together. "I know." She saw the quizzical look on Patrick's face. "He…" She searched for the right word. "Knew things," she finally said. "About me. About Brady and me," she added. If her brother was surprised, he gave no indication. "Things he couldn't have known unless he'd installed some kind of surveillance equipment there." The look on her brother's face told her that if Josh wasn't already dead, he would have killed the man with his own bare hands. Patience found herself comforting him. "It's over, Patrick."

Squaring her shoulders, she threaded her fingers through Brady's. The latter looked surprised, then smiled at her.

"Yeah." Patrick spat the word out. Then, because he was a policeman, born and bred, he caught hold of himself. When he asked her, "Are you up to coming down to the station and giving us a statement?" his voice was milder, more in control.

Patience nodded. She wanted to tell the story while the details were still fresh in her mind. She wanted to make sure that no blame whatsoever could fall on Brady. And then she wanted very much to forget any of this ever happened.

Her fingers tightened around Brady's hand as she followed her brother out of the house.

Because she was one of their own, the detectives conducting the interview at the precinct tried to make it as painless as possible for her. Even so, it was difficult for Patience to go over the events. Difficult to believe that it was finally behind her. The bruises on her arm where Josh had held her were only now beginning to form, but eventually they would fade.

She had no idea how long it would take for the impression he'd left on her soul to fade.

As she told the particulars of her experience, she watched members of her family enter the squad room. It seemed to her that every Cavanaugh had shown up at the precinct the moment they'd received word about what had happened.

Even Janelle came, to assure both her and Brady that as far as the D.A.'s office was concerned, this was a justifiable shooting and that the case was open and shut. There would be no repercussions and a commendation would be placed in Brady's file for acting cool under fire.

"Cool under fire," he mocked, shaking his head when things had finally died down at the precinct and he was allowed to take her home. "If they only knew."

These were his first words since before she'd given her statement to Detective Warner. Brady had seemed to all but withdraw into himself; something that had left her feeling uneasy because she had no way of being able to read that. No way of knowing what it meant.

Relieved to have him finally talking to her, she shifted in the patrol car and glanced at him. "If only they knew what?"

He spared her a look as he took the corner. His heart felt as if it were permanently lodged in his throat.

"That I was shaking inside," he told her, his voice low and betraying nothing. "That the second I realized what was going on, I was scared to death."

"Scared? You?" The word seemed incongruous with who and what Brady was. She'd doubted that he had any idea what the word fear meant.

"Scared," he repeated. "Me." So badly that his hands had felt like chunks of ice, unable to move swiftly enough to save her.

"You were afraid that he was going to kill you?"

"Hell, I didn't care about that, I was afraid he was going to kill you." And that would have been intolerable to him. He realized that now more than ever. Pulling up in front of her clinic, he yanked up the hand brake and turned to look at her. Almost hesitantly, he touched her hair. "I couldn't live in a world without you."

She thought of the way it had ended between them this morning. And that she'd been afraid that it was permanently over. "I got the impression that you could. Easily."

"Why? Because I walked away?"

Her mouth curved just a little. He'd saved her and no matter what happened, he was always going to be her hero. "That might have had something to do with it."

Didn't she understand why he'd done that? Why he wished he could still stand by his actions? But he couldn't because he knew he couldn't live his life without her. "That was because I didn't want to mess up your life."

Her eyes held his. Her smile deepened, delving into his soul. "Too late."

"Yeah, I know." He sighed, shaking his head. There was no denying what he felt, so he might as well own up to it. And throw himself on her mercy. "At least for me. No matter where I go, you'll always be inside of me."

She made no attempt to hide the spark of pleasure that had taken hold. Patience ran her hand along his chest, as if to take stock of it.

"Small space." She raised her eyes to his. "I'd rather be next to you instead of inside of you."

Brady got out of the car and rounded the hood until he was at the passenger door. Opening it for her, he took her hand and brought her to him. He was in so deep, he couldn't even begin to tread water.

"You know, I still don't have a clue how to make a relationship work."

Not waiting for an invitation, she fit herself against him, her body neatly filling the hollows of his. "Well, saving me from getting killed by a stalker buys you a lot of grace."

He liked holding her like this. Liked feeling her warmth spreading out along his skin. "Does it?"

To him, her eyes looked as if they were dancing. "You bet."

He'd never said the words to anyone before, never felt the least bit inclined to even entertain the possibility that he might feel this way about anyone. But he did. Now. About her. "I love you, you know."

Brady had all but whispered the words to her. She had to strain to hear them, and struggled now to convince herself that she wasn't dreaming. That she hadn't just wished them into existence.

"No," she told him quietly, her eyes raised to his, "I didn't."

Her statement left him stunned. "How could you not know?"

Typical man, she thought, her heart swelling as love filled every tiny crack, every space. "Maybe because you didn't say anything. A girl likes to hear those kinds of things."

He closed his arms around her, holding her tightly. Loving her even more so. "What else does a girl like to hear?"

She surprised him by shaking her head. "Oh, no, I can't put words into your mouth. You're on your own here, Coltrane."

Pausing to think, he blew out a breath. "That's what I'm afraid of."

Her body heated even more as she threaded her

fingers through his. "You don't ever have to be afraid, Brady. Not of me."

He wasn't afraid of her, he was afraid, at bottom, of rejection. It was better not to know than to suffer ultimate rejection, but he knew that he'd passed that point of no return. He needed her in his life. Permanently. The right way.

So he took his courage in his hand, something that had always been a given before, something he never explored until this very moment, and asked, "If I asked you to marry me…?"

"Why don't you try it and see what happens?"

There was encouragement in her voice. Or was he misreading it? "Patience Cavanaugh, will you marry me?"

Unable to hold it back any longer, she grinned even as she tried to hedge a second longer. "Can Tacoma be the ring bearer?"

Relief swirled through his chest. He'd jumped over the highest hurdle in his life—and cleared it. "King might get jealous."

"We could have both."

He pressed a kiss to her neck and heard her sigh. The beat of the heart that was lodged in his throat accelerated. "Is that a yes?"

She took his face between her hands and just looked at him. Loving him so much, it hurt. "That is most definitely a yes. I love you, Braden Coltrane.

I have for a while now.'' She saw the furrow in his brow and smoothed it out with her fingers. ''What?''

He had his doubts. Doubts that she wouldn't regret this. There were so many pitfalls, so many mistakes that could be made. But the greatest of mistakes would be if he'd let her go.

''You know, I don't know the first thing about making a marriage work, either, but I'll do whatever it takes to make you happy.'' It was a pledge, a promise he meant to keep.

Damn, but she'd really struck the jackpot this time. ''Just be, Brady,'' she whispered. ''Just be.''

''I can do that,'' he told her just before he lowered his head and kissed her.

*   *   *   *   *

If you enjoyed ALONE IN THE DARK,
you'll love Marie Ferrarella's next romance,
THE M.D.'S SURPRISE FAMILY,
available December 2004
from Silhouette Special Edition.

Bestselling fantasy author Mercedes Lackey turns traditional fairy tales on their heads in the land of the Five Hundred Kingdoms.

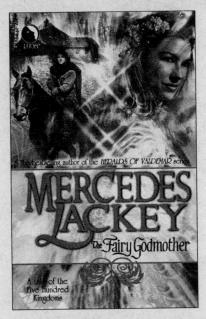

Elena, a Cinderella in the making, gets an unexpected chance to be a Fairy Godmother. But being a Fairy Godmother is hard work and she gets into trouble by changing a prince who is destined to save the kingdom, into a donkey—but he really deserved it!

Can she get things right and save the kingdom? Or will her stubborn desire to teach this ass of a prince a lesson get in the way?

On sale November 2004.
Visit your local bookseller.

Coming in December 2004

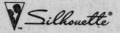
Silhouette®

Desire®

and
Alexandra Sellers
bring you another book in her popular miniseries

Powerful sheikhs born to rule and destined
to find their princess brides....

SONS
OF THE
DESERT

Don't miss...

THE ICE MAIDEN'S SHEIKH
(SD #1623)

**Desperate to keep her royal status a secret,
Jalia Shahbazi refuses to fall under the spell of the
magnetic Latif Abd al Razzaq Shahin. But as they search
the mountains together, looking for her missing cousin,
Jalia finds it's easier to ignore the fact that she's a
princess than her feelings for the mysterious sheikh.**

Available at your favorite retail outlet.

If you enjoyed what you just read,
then we've got an offer you can't resist!

Take 2 bestselling
love stories FREE!

Plus get a FREE surprise gift!